THE TRUMPESTIAD

A SAD AMERICAN COMEDY

(A THREE ACT PLAY)

Richard A. Pundt

ARCHWAY
PUBLISHING

Archway Publishing books may be ordered through booksellers or by contacting:

Archway Publishing
1663 Liberty Drive
Bloomington, IN 47403
www.archwaypublishing.com
844-669-3957

Interior Image Credit: Clayton Chambers

ISBN: 978-1-4808-9685-7 (sc)
ISBN: 978-1-4808-9686-4 (hc)
ISBN: 978-1-4808-9687-1 (e))

Library of Congress Control Number: 2020918674

Print information available on the last page.

Archway Publishing rev. date: 10/13/2020

CONTENTS

FOREWORD

For centuries Greek Tragedies have found a place in the libraries and the hands of people across the globe. One popular such tragedy is the Greek play of *Alcestis,* who was the wife of the Thessalian king, known for his hospitality, King Admetus. The king, who treated the Greek God Apollo to great favor when Apollo had been exiled from Olympus, is granted the right to live past his "time of death," if he can find a substitute for him when the time comes. Although King Admetus cannot find a substitute, his wife, Queen Alcestis, agrees to go in his place. Later Heracles brings Alcestis back from the underworld.

Perhaps, one of the best renditions of this story, aside from the original by Euripides, is the three-act play on the subject by Thornton Wilder. In Wilder's play, *The Alcestiad,* the story does not change; however, the dramatic portrayal is vividly told. Interesting dialogue is presented in *The Alcestiad* relative to the presence of Apollo, the god of healing, song and the sun, when he is disguised as a herdsman. What is clearly puzzling is why the god Apollo would allow one member of a devoted marriage die for the other if Apollo truly loved them both, which was supposedly the case. But, of course, it is a Greek tragedy. As in all of Wilder's works, the story is refreshingly retold.

Thornton Wilder is so well-respected and his writings so well-regarded that people will often show great affinity for his work and for him. For example, the famous actor Gene Wilder (real name Jerome Silberman) thought so much of Thornton Wilder that Silberman chose the name Wilder because of his admiration for Wilder and his work, *Our Town*. He chose the name Gene from another stage character. Since I, too, am fond of Thornton Wilder's writings, it is fair to say that Wilder's *Alcestiad* influenced the concept for *The Trumpestiad*.

The Trumpestiad, was the result of my rereading of *The Alcestiad*. It is my intention to present through *The Trumpestiad* a satirical rendition of the circumstances placed in motion by the Donald Trump Administration that deserved a visit from the Greek God, Apollo. So, now, as always, the Greeks have their Greek Tragedies, and we Americans have our "Sad American Comedy."

As an additional point, a re-reading of *The Oresteia* was helpful to me in the sense that it was the goddess Athena who devised the first known jury of twelve when she was called upon by Orestes and, likely Apollo, to come to the aid of Orestes when, after he had been set free from the Furies by Apollo, the Furies again find Orestes. The Furies initially hunted Orestes down for murdering his mother, Clytemnestra, who, in turn had murdered Orestes father, Agamemnon. The string of murders were all matters of revenge for multiple triangles of love along with the intervention of the gods. Athena set up the first trial by jury as she determined that violent retaliation must end. It happened that Athena, herself, broke a tie vote by the jury, therefore, Orestes was not killed. From that point forward, at least in Greek Mythology, it was determined that all trials were to be settled in a court by a jury instead of allowing for personal vengeance.

Perhaps because of the principles of justice set forth in the *Oresteia*, and the knowledge of our Founding Fathers of historic concepts of justice, trials in the United States render justice through a jury of peers. In *The Trumestiad*, Apollo is inadvertently contacted by Donald Trump through a misspelled tweet. When

Apollo arrives at the White House, he overhears an argument between Donald Trump and Uncle Sam. Ultimately, Apollo decides to call forth twelve of the attendees at a Trump rally to be formed as a jury that must determine whether the Pillars of Truth can be returned from Hell where they were sent by Donald Trump.

CAST

APOLLO .... An Elegant and Godlike Presence
DEARTH .... An Ambivalent Blandly Dressed Entity
TRUMP .... An Orange Blob with a Yellow Top
KELLY ANN .... A Blond Woman of Middle Age
UNCLE SAM .... Normal Figure with Top Hat & Striped Pants
FOX .... A Sneaky, Cunning, and Rapid Creature
MOSCOW MITCH .... A Small Dark Figure with a Ushanka
FRUITY RUDY .... A Small Twisted Figure with Bulging Eyes
BLACK BARR .... A Stupid and Overbearing Attorney General
HADES .... The Greek God in Control of Hell
ETHICS .... A Beautiful and Pure Creature
INTEGRITY .... A Beautiful and Pure Creature
HONESTY .... A Beautiful and Pure Creature
LOYALTY .... A Beautiful and Pure Creature
COURTESY .... A Beautiful and Pure Creature
REVERENCE .... A Beautiful and Pure Creature
HONOR .... A Beautiful and Pure Creature
JUSTICE .... A Beautiful and Pure Creature
JOE CONSTRUCT .... A Middle-Aged Construction Worker
Dr. ALTHEA MEDIC .... An Intelligent Young Woman M.D.
MR. BIG JEANS .... A Seasoned and Rugged Farmer
MISS LILITH RULER .... A Bright Young Elementary Teacher
EARNEST CRAFT .... A Labor Union Worker
FATHER DOUBT .... An Elderly Man of the Cloth

ACT ONE

As the curtain opens, the scene starts with what was a beautiful and sunny day on the south lawn of the U. S. White House in Washington D.C. As the sun begins to set in the west to the left of the stage, the White House appears in a yellowish hue in the background of the south lawn that opens to the audience. As the sun casts a yellowish-white light upon the White House, there is a rustling in a grouping of bushes near a tree to the left front of the stage. A Party Awning trimmed in white and red to the right front of the stage is displayed with a campaign sign that in large red letters reads, "Trump-Taking America Back.".

Off to the left of the stage, Apollo, the ancient Greek God, who is dressed in a flowing and full-length white robe with a bright blue sash over his left shoulder, partially appears near the upper part of the open curtain to the left of the stage. Initially, he peers out over the scene with his one hand shielding his eyes as he assesses the situation. He then starts to descend while partly obscured by the

1

curtain and appears to float down along the curtain by a tree near the bushes and lands on the lawn below. As he reaches the level of the stage, he starts to manipulate a handheld electronic devise which he carefully examines and bewilderingly shakes his head as he holds the electronic device up toward the light.

Apollo takes several steps toward the center of the stage but stops to look inquisitively at the audience when he hears the rustling in the nearby bushes. Diverting his attention from the audience and toward the bushes, he observes an ambivalent and bland figure dressed in various shades of gray and brown struggling to free break free of the bushes. Apollo raises his free hand, points to the bushes and issues a command in a most authoritative voice.

APOLLO:

Bushes…I direct you to release whomever you have trapped there!

(Immediately, the ambivalent and bland figure, stumbles forth from the bushes. As the figure attempts to gain his balance, he drops an electronic device and is startled to see Apollo. He backs away from the bushes while grasping his electronic device from the ground. He then addresses Apollo, who stands over the figure in a commanding position.)

DEARTH:

Good Heavens, Apollo! What brings you here from your heavenly abode… to, of all places, the White House in America? Why aren't you in Greece where you belong? They can surely use your help right now.

APOLLO:

Dearth? I'm surprised to see you. You, who are lacking in presence of substance, and typically deficient in every way, now present a viable image? Although you are a noun, it is indeed a rare event to see you personified. As Apollo, I must know the meaning of this. I hereby command you to tell me what you doing here? Furthermore, why have you taken the form of a living entity?

DEARTH:

True. Typically, I represent the lack of anything substantial. I'm not sure that I have ever been personified before. However, I received a tweet on my electronic device here. It said, <u>RT@WhiteHouse. Dearth should come to all Non-Trumpians. Rally Tonite at White House. So, here I am.</u>

APOLLO:

Now, that is odd. I too received a tweet from this location and my tweet said...here, let me bring it up.

(Apollo fiddles with his electronic device.)

Here it is. It was also a tweet from the White House. It said, <u>RT@ WhiteHouse. It's just Fake News again! Don't they realize that their great president has saved the country. I beseech Apollo to come with me.</u>

DEARTH:

Listen! Someone is coming.

APOLLO:

Let's step back by the bushes. I'll create a fog so that whomever comes will not be able to see us.

Apollo and Dearth step back. Apollo waives his free hand in the air before him. A cottonlike mist appears, drops from above, and settles between where Apollo and Dearth are standing near the bushes and the main part of the stage. Soon, the back entrance to the White House opens. A blond person emerges with what appears to be a perpetual but distorted smile. She opens her arms as if to embrace the entire day.

KELLY ANN:

What a beautiful day! This will be a good day for a rally. Here at the White House no one will need to worry about a COVID-19 virus or anything else. We Trumpians are immune to everything. Well, almost everything. Except for Democrats. We're immune to everything but Democrats and, oh, I almost forgot, those RINO and LINCOLN Republicans. The Democrats couldn't even convict on the basis of that stupid impeachment effort. And, those RINO and LINCOLN Republicans were no help. But now, we are free. Free to do as we please. The President is so happy. He's immune to everything. That's why I like him so much. Why, I'll say anything for him. And, boy do I know how to cover for him. I know that I am good at what I do. Why, I'm probably immune too. Although it probably doesn't matter since I will soon be leaving this wonderful post.

As Kelly Ann is reminiscing, an enormously large orange blob with artificially colored yellow hair and wearing a large blue suit and extra-long red necktie ambles out of the door of the White House and uses a form of pseudopodia that seems to absorb the ground as it waddles toward Kelly Ann. While he engages in its waddle style walk normally displayed by those with serious weight problems, the figure moves toward Kelly Ann. He addresses her in his unnaturally elevated and airy voice.

TRUMP:

Hi Kelly Ann. This is a new blue suit. Rallies are fun. People like us. We are wonderful. They know that. Fake news has not been invited. We can say what we want. Are there extra caps? Do we have enough? For tonight's speech, I have a surprise. I will include a complex sentence.

KELLY ANN:

Hello, Mr. President. You're right, tonight's rally will be fun since there will be only friends. There will be no press, except for the FOX. The FOX likes us. Tonight, we don't need to worry about the news media. Are you sure that you want to include a complex sentence? It might be too much for you to worry about, and it might be too much for your supporters to understand. We don't want to get them angry. The supporters understand the simple sentences. They like simple things. In fact, they like to have the simple things repeated over and over. None of them are into anything complex. I would not use a complex sentence.

TRUMP:

They like me. They like my rallies. Since the virus, rallies are hard to do. But the forever Trumpers like rallies. They want me to rally. They want me to run. I will run. Run. Run. Run. I can run.

KELLY ANN:

Yes, Mr. President. You can run. You always run hard. They do like you. Your fans…er…I mean, supporters will do anything for you. They believe.

TRUMP:

They do believe. They like me. I can run. I run hard. I run a lot. I'm good at running. I do run fast. My tweets run fast. Trumpers often say: Run Donald, run. Run. Run. Run. That should be my slogan. Run Donald, run.

KELLY ANN:

Yes, Mr. President. By the way, was there an earlier tweet about the rally?

TRUMP:

Probably. I'm sure that I did many. I like to tweet. It's fun. I get to tell people what to do. I order with my tweets. I even fire with tweets.

KELLY ANN:

Have you considered using the spell check?

TRUMP:

What's that?

KELLY ANN:

Never mind. You realized that the FOX will be here?

TRUMP:

The FOX is my advisor. The FOX likes me. The FOX is good.

KELLY ANN:

What about the Steve the Miller? Will he be here? I often have trouble seeing him.

TRUMP:

He's here now. He is always with me. I have him under my coat. He can come out later. He likes it when its dark.

KELLY ANN:

What about the KIDS? Will they be here? I don't always see them; although I know they are around somewhere. I see notes from them and I know that they are in and out of the White House a lot.

TRUMP:

They won't be here. They are too busy. They do world affairs. They also handle the many wonderful businesses. There are many wonderful businesses. We own many businesses. The businesses are good. The KIDS know things. They are almost as smart as me.

KELLY ANN:

Yes, Mr. President. They are almost as smart as you.

TRUMP:

Is your uncle coming? I really don't like him. He's too showy. He always tries to take attention away from me. He's just a show off. If he's going to use colorful clothes, he should try one of my ties.

KELLY ANN:

Yes. He's coming. Please be nice to him. He's been around a long time. He believes that he should be here. In fact, he's coming early since he wants to talk to you privately.

TRUMP:

Do I have to? He's a show boat. Always taking attention away from me. Besides, I don't think he likes me. He tries to tell me what to do. Plus, he always tries to direct the attention to himself instead of me.

KELLY ANN:

Shh. I think I hear him coming now. Please be nice. He's our uncle.

From the right of the stage, near the Party Awning steps a tall man dressed in a large faded white top hat circled with a blue band with stars, along with a white shirt, a red bow tie, a blue coat coupled with red and white striped pants and white shoes. The tall man stops to look at the awning, looks at the audience and shakes his head. He then ambles over to where Trump and Kelly Ann are standing. He begins to speak in his low authoritative voice.

UNCLE SAM:

Good afternoon Kelly Ann. Hello Donald. I hope it's not an imposition; however, I need a few minutes to discuss something with you, Donald. Would you excuse us Kelly Ann? I need to have a private discussion with Donald before the rally.

KELLY ANN:

No problem. I have some last-minute preparations to do. See you later.

Kelly Ann stands on her toes, kisses Uncle Sam on the cheek. She then turns and walks to the White House to continue preparations for the rally. Trump looks at Uncle Sam then crosses his arms in front of his chest and begins to pout while addressing Uncle Sam.

TRUMP:

What do you want Sam? This is not another lecture, I hope.

UNCLE SAM:

No lecture. I just want to know if you'll go with me. It's high time that you listen to me. You need to come with me since your presence will be required. So much must be done to correct the things that you have done over the past few years. I certainly hope that it is not too late for us to make things right. We should really go now.

TRUMP:

Go where? Wherever it is, I can't go. I have a rally that will start soon.

UNCLE SAM:

We need to go to see Hades.

TRUMP:

Where? Who? Whatever, I'm not going.

UNCLE SAM:

He's the master of the afterlife. The underworld. It's like Hell.

TRUMP:

Why would I go? You go. It's a dumb idea. What would be the purpose?

UNCLE SAM:

Bluntly, a lot has gone to Hell lately. The Coronavirus is out of control. Because of your failure to show any leadership regarding the COVID-19 outbreak, we've lost more lives than World War I, or the Viet Nam War, or the Korean War.

TRUMP:

So? It is what it is. Is that why you're here to complain again?

UNCLE SAM:

There's more. Much more. You've driven the Pillars of Truth to Hell. Because of you, we've lost the Pillars of Truth. That is most egregious.

TRUMP:

The Pillars of Blah, Blah, Blah.

UNCLE SAM:

The Pillars of Truth.

TRUMP:

Don't care about them.

UNCLE SAM:

You should. There are eight key elements that support the Pillars of Truth. We've lost them during your presidency. The Pillars of Truth have gone to Hell. We no longer have any "Ethics." There is no "Integrity." "Honesty" has been gone for a long time. "Loyalty," "Courtesy," "Reverence," "Honor," and "Justice" have all gone to Hell, as well. We need to go there to see if we can bring them back. You need to go with me to see for yourself.

TRUMP:

Don't look at me. I don't control them. It's not my fault.

UNCLE SAM:

But it is your fault. You paid them no heed when they crossed your path. You paid them no respect. You have ignored their presence and what they have represented for years in America. You're responsible for what happened to them. The least you could do is to come with me. We need desperately to get them back. Forget the rally and come with me. After all, you're responsible for them going to Hell.

TRUMP:

No. You go. I don't care where they've gone. I'm doing a rally. Period.

UNCLE SAM:

You can't do a rally at the White House.

TRUMP:

I don't see why I can't. So many of the state governors and city mayors are refusing to let us do a rally because of the distancing and masks they are requiring due to the COVID-19. I'm the President. I should do what I want. I want a rally; so, I should be able to have a rally. That's important to my fans. It's important to me, and besides, I'm the President. I can just do it. See the sign over by the awning? It says to take America back. Only I can do that. It's because I am the greatest president ever.

UNCLE SAM:

You're not the greatest president. You're the worst. You're right about one thing though.

TRUMP:

See, I am right. I'm right about so many things.

UNCLE SAM:

The only thing that you are right about is taking the country back. Way back! You're moving the country in the wrong direction and backwards. Just cancel the rally and come with me to see Hades. It's all your fault that the Pillars of Truth have gone to Hell. You should remember. You sent them there.

TRUMP:

Stop blaming. I'm the President. I have all the power. I can send the Pillars of Truth to Hell if I want. They were just in the way. They were always trying to tell me what to do. I just knew you were going to bring trouble.

UNCLE SAM:

I blame you for what you did. You're the reason we no longer have Ethics, Integrity, Honesty, Loyalty, Courtesy, Reverence, Honor, or Justice.

TRUMP:

I really don't care! Just as I told Kelly Ann. I knew that you'd bring trouble and ruin the mood. Besides, I don't like those Pillars. They were always complaining. Just like you. So, what if I sent them to Hell? As far as I'm concerned, Sam, you can go there too. In fact, that's a good idea. You can go to Hell.

UNCLE SAM:

You are the one who drove the Pillars out. Let me give you some examples. You told your attorney Cohen to cover up the Moscow Tower deal and other business dealings with Russia. Then you lied and denied dealing with Russia, or that you tried to set up business dealings with Russia.

TRUMP:

So what? Those were my business dealings. It was my business.

UNCLE SAM:

Well, that's the problem. You made it your business instead of the country's concern. When you lied about it, you were obstructing an investigation. When you're the President, the public needs to know about your business dealings, especially with Russia. Then what about your security advisor Flynn and his ties to the Russians, including Kislyak? Also, what about Flynn's relationship with Putin? Kislyak is a career Russian diplomat who was looking for an edge against you, and Putin is the devious former head of Russian intelligence. They are just trying to capitalize on your weaknesses and your greed for wealth.

TRUMP:

I don't believe that. Kislyak is a nice guy. So is Putin. He's a nice guy too. They both like me. They told me so. They just want to be friends. They wouldn't lie to me. It was that damn Comey and the U.S. intelligence community that were trying to make a fake security issues about things that were none of their business.

UNCLE SAM:

Comey was the head of the FBI. He was concerned about the Russians undermining the U.S. and trying to get a compromising position on you. You tried to get Comey to look the other way regarding Flynn. That was considered obstruction by quite a number of people.

TRUMP:

There's that obstruction thing again. Is that all you think about? Comey was a grand-stander. Just like you. He refused to show loyalty to me. Just like you. I was his boss. I'm your boss. I just asked Comey to let the Flynn investigation go. You should too. Nothing wrong with that.

UNCLE SAM:

Wrong. Once again, that's obstruction of justice. The Office of President has certain standards; or is supposed to have standards. As President, you can't ask the Director of the FBI to forget about a criminal investigation involving national security. Also, you can't ask the Deputy National Security Advisor to make up stuff about Flynn and Kislyak. You are not a mafia boss. You can't disregard the law. As President, you are supposed to follow the law. You need to be an example of integrity.

TRUMP:

I'm more powerful than a Mafia Boss. Just ask Fruity Rudy.

UNCLE SAM:

Fruity Rudy is a terrible example. I'll ignore your statement for everyone's sake. Additionally, you cannot direct the leaders of the intelligence agencies to make public statements that are not true.

TRUMP:

Why not? As President, I can do anything.

UNCLE SAM:

No, you can't. Asking members of the intelligence community to try to get Comey to stop an investigation is obstruction of justice pure and simple. You are wearing me out. You really need to go with me to see Hades.

TRUMP:

I'm not going to see Hades. Besides, I can fire anyone I want. In fact, if I could fire you, I would. I think I'll have an investigation done regarding you. I need to find out why you're always around.

UNCLE SAM:

You can't fire anyone you want. Not if it means obstructing justice. Firing someone like the FBI Director because he wouldn't stop an investigation of a guy who was improperly conferring with the Russians was improper. That was wrong and your reason was wrong. Then you complicated matters when you tried to terminate the Special Counsel or at least tried others to terminate him. Again, that's obstruction of justice.

TRUMP:

As President, I can obstruct anything I want. I can fire anyone I want. I fired a lot of people on my T.V. show. Just ask anybody. For example, ask Cory Lewandowski about the Russian investigation; he'll tell you they had nothing to do with the campaign.

UNCLE SAM:

No. I can't believe that. In fact, you were wrong in asking a former campaign manager to deliver a message to then Attorney General Sessions to publicly announce that the Special Counsel investigation would be confined to future election interference, and that Sessions should disregard his recusal from the investigation and state for a fact that the Russians were not involved in the campaign. Sessions was attempting to follow the law. You should have done what he did and you should have followed the law. You knew there was a grand jury investigation.

TRUMP:

Wait! Wait! You're talking too fast and saying too much. Besides, there was no evidence in regard to whatever you're saying.

UNCLE SAM:

You know that's not true. There was plenty of evidence. There were emails and you tried to prevent the disclosure of those emails. Do I need to remind you about the emails concerning the Trump Tower meeting? You also directed your staff to not publicly disclose information about that meeting. More obstruction.

TRUMP:

Will you get off this obstruction thing? I'm tired of hearing about it. You are really beginning to annoy me. I think I'm going to fire you. I'm the President and I can do anything that I want. Here, you're fired! How do you like that? If you are concerned about emails, check Hillary's.

UNCLE SAM:

That's nonsense. You can't fire me. I'm an American institution. Plus, there's much more we need to discuss. For example, you lied when you said that you didn't know about the Trump Tower meeting. And then you...

TRUMP:

That's enough. Nothing ever came of the investigation by the Special Counsel that involved me. I was exonerated. Just ask Bad Barr the Attorney General who looked over the Mueller Report. Bad Barr didn't find anything wrong with what I did. He didn't see anything in the Mueller Report that was against me. Besides, the Congress later tried to impeach me and never mentioned these so-called obstruction matters that the Special Counsel discussed. That's because I was exonerated. I am above the law. I'm the President.

UNCLE SAM:

That's the problem. You're the President and you have no respect for the office you hold. By the way, you were never exonerated by the Special Counsel or anyone else. Congress didn't try to impeach you. They did impeach you. You were impeached. You just weren't convicted by the Senate because your friend, Moscow Mitch, would not allow any evidence or witnesses to be presented at the trial in the Senate.

TRUMP:

Why don't you just ask Fruity Rudy, Bad Barr, or Moscow Mitch? They're going to be here for the rally. They're coming early. We are going to make our plans for at least four more years.

UNCLE SAM:

Well, if they're coming, let's have them come with us to see Hades. Fruity Rudy and Moscow Mitch have been advisors to you and, no doubt, have something to do with the Pillars of Truth going to Hell.

TRUMP:

Well, whatever. They are good advisors and so is the FOX. Without them, I wouldn't have the help I need. They have been very helpful. Lots of help.

UNCLE SAM:

Help? Really? So, is it a fair statement to say that they helped send the Pillars of Truth to Hell? It's my guess that each of them along with your close friend THE FOX all did their best to assist you in sending the Pillars of Truth to Hell.

TRUMP:

Are you finished? I need to get ready for the rally. Plus, those guys you just named are going to be here soon so we can plan for the rally. You can go!

UNCLE SAM:

If you're referring to Moscow Mitch, Fruity Rudy, FOX, and Black Barr, I'll wait. If you won't go with me to see Hades, maybe they will. After all, they've each contributed to the banishing of the Pillars of Truth to Hell. Clearly, each of them has done their part to drive Ethics Integrity, Honesty, Loyalty, Courtesy, Reverence,

Honor, and Justice to Hell. It is critical that the Pillars of Truth be returned for the sake of the country.

TRUMP:

It's just like I told Kelly Ann. You're nothing but trouble. You can go to Hell.

UNCLE SAM:

That's where I'm going. As I said, you need to come with me. Someone needs to go there in order to bring the Pillars of Truth back. I was hoping that you would go and apologize to Hades. He needs to know that it was a mistake for the Pillars to be driven to Hell. That's why it is imperative that Hades hear from you and that, in your own words, you tell him that the Pillars of Truth were never destined to be driven to Hell. You need to confess and admit that you've been wrong about so many things. Perhaps if you're humble, Hades will release the Pillars of Truth.

TRUMP:

I told you that I'm not going. Period. I've never done anything wrong, ever. Everything that I do is right. I only do good things. Just ask Moscow Mitch, Fruity Rudy, FOX and Bad Barr. They will all tell you how good I am at everything I do. I never met anyone as good as I am. Even all of my fans think so. After all they overwhelmingly elected me to be the President. It was clearly the biggest landslide victory ever.

UNCLE SAM:

No, it wasn't! You lost the popular vote. You are not as popular as you would like to think. Of course, Fruity Rudy, Moscow Mitch,

Bad Bar, and THE FOX will stick up for you. Maybe, they can go with me to face Hades.

TRUMP:

No. I need them here for the rally. If they agree with me, then so do the Trumpians. That's the whole point of the rally. They all like to see me.

UNCLE SAM:

If you don't go and they don't go, who can go with me to plead with Hades. Hades needs to know that it was wrong for you to try to get A.G. Sessions to reverse his recusal. He needs to know that you didn't mean to order your attorneys to deny that you tried to fire the Special Counsel. He needs to know that you didn't mean to have your attorneys lie to the media. He needs to know that you lied about Michael Flynn and Paul Manafort. He needs to know that you lied about the various extramarital affairs and the pay offs to the women involved. He needs to know whether you told attorney Cohen to lie or whether you tried to prevent Mr. Cohen from telling the truth to the Special Counsel.

TRUMP:

You're really getting on my nerves. Why don't you just leave and go to Hell.

UNCLE SAM:

If that's going to be your attitude, I'll wait until your friends arrive. Maybe I can get them to realize what has happened to the Pillars of Truth. Perhaps they'll see how important it is for Hades to release the Pillars of Truth from Hell. Maybe they can apologize for you, since you are either unwilling or incapable of apologizing yourself.

TRUMP:

If you're looking for an apology, you'll never get it from me. Why are you calling for Moscow Mitch, Fruity Rudy, Bad Barr, or the FOX to go with you? If it's for an apology, I doubt that you'll get an apology from them either. By the way, it doesn't look like you will need to wait too long, for here they come.

Entering the stage from just beyond the bushes where Apollo and Dearth are standing behind the veil, are Moscow Mitch with a large black Ushanka bobbing on his head as he walks, Fruity Rudy with an erratic stride and bulging eyes that dart from side to side, Black Barr whose rotund presence causes a waddle between left and right as he walks, and the FOX whose sly and cunning moves emulate a weaving gait. They cross from left stage to center right of the stage to where Trump and Uncle Sam are standing to the left of the red and white awning.

TRUMP:

Welcome my friends. I'm happy that you came early. Perhaps you guys can help me. I can't get rid of Uncle Sam. He came here with a crazy idea that I would follow him into Hell to see Hades.

BLACK BARR:

What in the Hell are you talking about? You, Sam, why don't you tell me?

FRUITY RUDY:

Yeah! Sam, why don't you tell us what the hell you are talking about?

UNCLE SAM:

You're both lawyers so you should understand. The Pillars of Truth have all gone to Hell under this administration. By this administration, I'm particularly referring to the President's actions; however, I am also referring to the actions of the four of you, as well.

FRUITY RUDY:

What Pillars of Truth. I've never heard of them. Is it something new?

UNCLE SAM:

You should have heard of them. Perhaps you don't remember them from law school. Perhaps, you were gone on the days they were discussed. To refresh your memory, let me at least mention them. They are: ETHICS, INTEGRITY, HONESTY, LOYALTY, COURTESY, REVERENCE, HONOR, and JUSTICE. They are the Pillars of Truth.

FRUITY RUDY:

Oh those. I've actually heard of them; but no one pays them any heed. I certainly don't. Under this administration, we've never really had any need for them. Did you say that they went somewhere? Where, did you say they went?

UNCLE SAM:

They've gone to Hell under this administration. I came here to insist that President Trump come with me to see if Hades would release them back to us so that we could once again function as we are supposed to under the Constitution.

BAD BARR:

We have no need for them any longer. We've suspended the Constitution. It was just getting in the way. We can do more without them and more without the Constitution in terms of ful-filling our agenda. As I have said publicly, History records what the winners do, and we're the winners.

MOSCOW MITCH:

Why Sir, A.G. Barr is correct. We certainly can suspend the Constitution. In fact, we have done it. As we say in Kentucky, when you hold the reins of power, it's a matter of control. We hold the reins and we control the power. And, as far as the Constitution is concerned, why, we have our own interpretation. There are some rich and powerful people who put us in office and since we hold those reins of power, we repay the rich and powerful with due consideration. That's the way they like to see government operate. Actually, there is really no need for a Constitution. Let's just say that it's been suspended. Ha. Ha. Ha.

UNCLE SAM:

You can't do that. The Constitution is there for a reason. It's for everyone.

MOSCOW MITCH:

Don't be so naive. The operation of government and the Constitution is open to interpretation by whomever is in power. Our interpretation is that the Constitution is simply superfluous to the way we choose to operate. However, there are a few provisions we like to cite when it suits us.

UNCLE SAM:

No, no, no. I must vehemently protest. I've been around a long time. In fact, a lot longer than any of you; and I can tell you that is not the way it is. The Constitution is a special document that was purposely written to protect all. I knew the founding fathers.

MOSCOW MITCH:

To hell with the Founding Fathers, sir. Today, there is a different philosophy that needs to be followed. Haven't you ever heard of Machiavelli? He has been called by many the father of political philosophy. According to him, a leader has the power to engage in whatever acts he deems necessary to govern. Whatever the leader decides is the rule. Why, the disposal of those who resist is even appropriate. As you may have noticed, we've done our best to eliminate dissent. Since I like to refer to myself as the "Grim Reaper," I can assure you that dissent has and will continue to be eliminated where and when it is necessary.

UNCLE SAM:

That's outrageous and an outright distortion of Machiavelli's *The Prince*. The founding fathers of the United States were fully aware of Machiavelli and his works. Our founding fathers wanted to be sure that the United States was not governed by a prince but by the people. The Constitution was purposely written, among other things, to be certain that there was no chance of a prince governing the people of the United States. The founding fathers did not want a tyrant who could engage in evil for the sake of political expediency and rule as he wished. Although Machiavelli wrote the *The Prince*, he was not actually advocating such unbridled rule, and...

MOSCOW MITCH:

That's a matter of interpretation. You have yours and we have ours. Our interpretation controls since we are in power. Sam, you no longer count.

TRUMP:

It's not "we" who are in power. I'm in power. Donald Trump is in power. Also, I am not a prince, I am a president, who really has the power of a king. I like that. The power of a king. In fact, I am king and what I say or tweet stands. I can hire or fire with a tweet. I can govern with a tweet. I have the power to do as I wish.

BAD BARR:

There might be some limitations or guidelines that you should follow and that's why you have me as your Attorney General. It is I who can help you navigate the Constitution and other laws. I can twist things better than most lawyers. I like to twist things, especially the law.

MOSCOW MITCH:

Now sir, don't forget the power of the Senate. I hold that power. You need me. With my control over the Senate, just the laws that we deem proper and useful will get passed. Nothing else will see the light of day. Just ask Nancy Pelosi.

FRUITY RUDY:

Also, don't forget why you have me. I can do more by being a quasi-operative for you. I am not bound by any rules. I can do more for you from the outside. I'm really a free agent. I like that. A special agent like Bond.

UNCLE SAM:

That's what happened in regard to Ukraine. A clear deviation from the law and all protocol. All of those actions were improper under the Constitution and that's why you were impeached, Mr. Trump. Fruity Rudy is a loose cannon. Everyone says so.

THE FOX:

I don't say so. Listen to all of you. None of you would be in the positions you're in if it were not for me. If you have traveled around the country to listen to the people who count, you would realize that I am the one. I have been the sly and cunning force who has helped each of you, except Sam, into the positions of power that you hold. Don't ever forget the power of the FOX. By the way Sam, you no longer have a voice, so why don't you just buzz off? The way we govern in the United States has passed you by. Now, we tell the people what to believe and what to do. You no longer have a purpose or a voice. Just leave!

UNCLE SAM:

No! I'm not leaving until I have an agreement from the President to go with me to see Hades in Hell and plead for the release of the Pillars of Truth.

THE FOX:

Truth? What an antiquated concept. The truth doesn't cut it anymore. The people don't want the truth. They just want to hear something that either makes them feel good about themselves or something that enrages their emotions. That's where I come in. I do the persuading.

UNCLE SAM:

No! That just cannot be the case. Not in the United States of America. There's a Constitution. There are laws. There is judicial precedent. There are rules. The people want to follow the Constitution, the rules and the judicial precedent. The reason the citizens of the United States are the envy of the world is because of all of these features that make the U. S. what it is.

THE FOX:

Not anymore. The Citizens have no idea what is good for them. They need to be told what to like and what to do. They need to be told what their rights are. The powerful and wealthy know best and they work with the FOX. The rich one percent get it and they got it. Get a handle on what is going on, Sam. The wealthy and the FOX control the country. That's the way it should be. The citizens are too busy enjoying their limited lives. They need leadership and that is what the wealthy and the FOX provide. The Constitution is passé. It applies where we say it applies and that's it. The judicial precedent is being changed into what we want. I alone have the power through all of the media outlets that I possess to change the way the people think. I have done that. All the other media outlets follow what I do. If I decide to give the President coverage on something, the other media outlets follow my lead. If I focus on an idea, the other media outlets follow my lead. I have an incredible following; and the other media outlets are envious. Along with the wealthy, I am in control.

MOSCOW MITCH:

Now sir, wait just a minute. Aren't you forgetting those of us who are elected officials? We actually control the country and what happens to the laws, the courts, the rules, and the way of life.

THE FOX:

Let's remember how you got to where you are. The wealthy and THE FOX put you into your position of power. Without the funds of the wealthy and the media influence that THE FOX provides, you would be nothing. That's true for the President, as well. Remember that.

TRUMP:

I don't like bickering. I'm the President not any of you. You owe me complete allegiance. I expect loyalty. Unconditional loyalty. Each of you needs to acknowledge the great job that I am doing. I am doing a fantastic job. No one has ever done as good a job as me. I deserve all the credit for that. In fact, I deserve the Nobel Prize. Also, I should be on Mt Rushmore. Someone should look into that. Maybe THE FOX can promote that. That would be something that we could discuss at the rally later today.

At this point the Trump entourage end their bickering, turn their backs on Uncle Sam and begin walking toward the rally. They continue to talk on their way. Uncle Sam urges them to stop.

UNCLE SAM:

Forget the rally. You shouldn't be doing a rally at the White House anyhow. With COVID-19 a reality, you should really be more careful. Please, you need to come with me.

In unison the Trump group turns and shake their heads and fists at Uncle Sam. Trump responds to Uncle Sam.

TRUMP:

Not! I've told you that I am not going. None of us are going. That would be a waste of time. Just get out of here. Can't you see that you are no longer welcome at this house. I told Kelly Ann that you're nothing but trouble. So, just go! The rest of you come with me so we can make our plans. We need to discuss the rally and raising some money.

UNCLE SAM:

What about you, Bad Barr? Surely, as the Attorney General, you should want to see the Pillars of Truth be released by Hades and back from Hell.

BAD BARR:

I don't think so. I kind of like things the way they are. We don't need them.

UNCLE SAM:

Well then, what about you Fruity Rudy? Any chance that you would at least try to come with me?

FRUITY RUDY:

Not a chance. I never cared for those stupid Pillars of Truth at all.

UNCLE SAM:

What about you, Moscow Mitch? For the people?

MOSCOW MITCH:

Not a chance Loser!

UNCLE SAM:

What about you, FOX? Any chance that you would go with me to bring…

THE FOX:

You have to know better than to ask. I helped put them in Hell. You're on your own SAM. There's not a chance in Hell. Heh. Heh. That I'd help you.

At this point TRUMP, BAD BARR, FRUITY RUDY, MOSCOW MITCH, and THE FOX go under the awning and start laughing at UNCLE SAM as he walks slowly and dejectedly to the left of the stage. As UNCLE SAM reaches the half-way point of the stage, the veil that APPOLO placed earlier between them slowly rises so that both APPOLO and DEARTH become visible to UNCLE SAM. Soon

Uncle Sam notices the presence of APPOLO and DEARTH. He stops abruptly and extends his arms outward in a push back motion and in disbelief. APPOLO and DEARTH cautiously approach Uncle Sam.

UNCLE SAM:

Who are you and what are you doing here?

APOLLO:

I am the Greek God, Apollo. I received a tweet. I was beseeched to come and it sounded important so, I came to find out. Did you send the tweet?

DEARTH:

I, too, received a tweet from this location. So, I came, as well.

UNCLE SAM:

Apollo, I am honored to meet you. Dearth, I'm surprised that I am even seeing you at all. I've never known of you having any substance. Let me tell you both that I did not send any tweet; however, I suspect that I know who did.

APOLLO:

Please tell me. It sounded urgent. I was beseeched. It's not often that a request comes to save an entire country. So, I came right away.

DEARTH:

The tweet I received said that I should come. So, I came.

UNCLE SAM:

May I see those tweets. Perhaps, yours first Apollo.

*Apollo presents his handheld device to UNCLE SAM and reads the
message out loud.*

APOLLO:

See, it reads: <u>RT@WhiteHouse. It's just Fake News again! Don't
they realize that their great president has saved the country. Big
Rally tonight! I beseech Apollo to come with me.</u>

UNCLE SAM:

It definitely came from President Trump. He is always either misspelling words or confusing the text of a message. No doubt you
probably were not aware of that problem. It's my guess that the
message was supposed to say: "…Big Rally tonight. My speech to
follow, so come with me." Because of Mr. Trump's reckless nature,
the message came out: "…Big Rally tonight. I beseech Apollo to
come with me." He was trying to say that a ***big speech to follow***
and not ***to beseech Apollo***. Frankly, and no offense; however, I
doubt that Mr. Trump even knows who you are, Apollo.

APOLLO:

Needless to say, I am offended and upset that this Mr. Trump
has taken me away from my beloved Greece and her people. I am
baffled that he does not know who I am.

UNCLE SAM:

Don't be. That's just an example of the reckless nature of Mr. Trump. So, you will probably want to leave and go back to Greece where you are recognized and appreciated.

APOLLO:

No, I don't think so. I over-heard your conversation with this Mr. Trump and his associates. I didn't realize that Mr. Trump had attempted to send the Pillars of Truth to Hell. I heard the distress in your voice and how you would like to have them back. I believe I can help you.

UNCLE SAM:

How could you help? Why would you help? There is no way that I could repay you.

APOLLO:

You will not need to repay me. Hades, the keeper of the underworld, is my uncle. I have a good relationship with him. He will listen to me. Besides, there is no way that the United States should exist without the presence of the Pillars of Truth. I will help you. In fact, I will personally escort you to see Hades.

UNCLE SAM:

I don't know how to thank you. It will be good to have the Pillars of Truth back where they belong. Thank you for this great offer.

DEARTH:

What about me. I, too, have a twitter message from Mr. Trump to be here. Let me show you Uncle Sam. Perhaps, you can make sense of my twitter message.

UNCLE SAM:

I will see if I can help. Let me see your twitter message

At this point DEARTH presents his handheld device and extends his arm so that UNCLE SAM can see the message while DEARTH reads it out loud.

DEARTH:

As you can see, it reads: RT@WhiteHouse. Dearth should come to all Non-Trumpians. Rally Tonite at White House. I don't know why Mr. Trump says that I should come to the White House.

UNCLE SAM:

That's easy. I'm sure it was a simple spelling error by Mr. Trump. No doubt, he meant to say that "death should come to all Non-Trumpians" and not that Dearth, should come to the rally.

DEARTH:

Oh. Good. That means I can go. I'm not sure I like being personified.

APOLLO:

No. I don't think so. I have a plan to make things right. It involves you Dearth. You will come with Uncle Sam and me to see Hades.

ACT TWO

The scene is set in Hell. Standing at the front of the stage, in a whitish-grey robe along with a scepter and horn of plenty at his belt is Hades, who manages the underworld. He is quite tall, supporting a full bluish-grey beard along with flaming blue hair and blueish grey skin which changes when he becomes angry at which point his hair turns orange and his skin turns red. Beside him is his three headed dog, Cerberus.

In the far background is a near replica of the United States White House, only it is finished in red instead of white and is flooded with red lighting. Standing between Hades and the large red replica of the White House in the background are eight women dressed in flowing white robes. The women, who are lined up behind Hades from left to right are: Ethics, who has a purple sash draped from her left shoulder to her right hip; Integrity, who has a green sash draped from her left shoulder to her right hip; Honesty, who has a white sash draped from her left shoulder to her right hip; Loyalty,

who has a Pink sash draped from her left shoulder to her right hip;
Courtesy, who has a yellow sash draped from her left shoulder to
her right hip; Reverence, who has a black sash draped from her left
shoulder to her right hip; Honor, who has a blue sash draped from
her left shoulder to her right hip; and Justice, who has a silver sash
draped from her left shoulder to her right hip.

To the left of the stage is the undergrowth of the bushes that were to
the left of the stage in Act One. To the right of the stage, where the
rally awning was in Act One, is an intensely burning fire that crack-
les and hisses. Apollo, Dearth, and Uncle Sam enter the stage from
the left at the location of the undergrowth. Hades turns to greet his
guests with a hardy laugh as he pounds his scepter on the ground.

HADES:

Well, well, well. What brings my illustrious nephew, Apollo, to
my hinterland? And, who may I ask, do you have with you at the
time of this rare visit?

At this point Apollo and Hades meet each other at mid stage and
give each other a strong embrace and look each other over from top
to bottom while smiling and shaking their heads.

APPOLO:

Greetings Hades! It's been too long. I trust that you've been well.

HADES:

How is my nephew? And how is your father?

APPOLO:

I'm well, thanks. My father is fine, as far as I know. He's always busy with one thing or another.

HADES:

So he is. Give Zeus my regards when you see him. Tell him to stop by.

APOLLO:

I will. I trust that all is well with you here in the Underworld.

HADES:

All is well. However, I have some guests who don't belong. It presents a real dilemma for me. Now, what brings you and your friends here?

APOLLO:

I am here on a mission. I have with me a gentleman known as Uncle Sam, the representative of the United States along with the personification of Dearth. Both of them are on the same mission as am I.

HADES:

Oh, I recognize Uncle Sam. In fact, I believe that there are eight radiant ladies from the United States here with me. I'll introduce them to you, momentarily, and I'm certain that Uncle Sam already knows them. But first, let me hear of your mission. As an observation, permit me to note that I have never seen the personification of Dearth. In fact, I never would have thought that it would be possible for the "lack of something" to be personified. How has this happened.

DEARTH:

It's never happened to me before. I was summoned to the White House of the United States by its president, a Donald Trump. I received a twitter message that stated "…may Dearth come to all non-Trumpians." So, as commanded, I came to a rally that was being prepared at the White House. I needed to find out what it meant. As it turns out, and according to Uncle Sam, there was a misspelling by Mr. Trump in regard to the twitter. Apparently, he meant to use the word "death" but mentioned "Dearth" instead. I thought that because of the mistake, I would be able to go; however, Apollo said he had plans for me and I must come with him to see you.

HADES:

With all of my wisdom, I have no idea what the purpose of Apollo's thinking must be. However, I do know that there is certainly much opportunity for Dearth here in Hell since many of earth's previous occupants, who are here now, lacked so much during their lives. Because they lacked so little direction, they ended up here in my domain. Many lacked character. Others lacked courage. Some lacked ethics, or integrity, or honesty, or loyalty, or comity, or reverence, or honor, or a sense of justice. The list just goes on and on. I can tell you something though. I do know who this President Donald Trump is. He will be expected as a permanent resident at a point in the future. He has many friends here. In fact, as you may have noticed, I have a replica of the White House behind you and it's appointed in red. I believe that Mr. Trump will like it since red seems to be one of his favorite colors. At least I have noticed that he likes red ties. As far as Dearth is concerned, let me assure you, Dearth, you have a permanent place here should you ever chose to come. Now let me turn my attention to my nephew, Apollo. Tell me Apollo, what is this mission you speak of?

APOLLO:

Like Dearth, I was invited to the rally at the White House. I, too, received a tweet from Donald Trump. In fact, I was beseeched to come. After discussing the tweet with Uncle Sam, it was apparent that Mr. Trump intended to tweet something entirely different. Nevertheless, since I was beseeched, I went to the White House. While I was at there, I overheard a conversation between Uncle Sam, here, and this President Trump along with some of Mr. Trump's associates. It turns out that Uncle Sam is distressed that the Pillars of Truth have been banished from the United States during the Trump Presidency. Apparently, the Pillars of Truth have been sent to Hell by President Trump and his associates. After listening to the conversation that Uncle Sam had with President Trump and the others, I made it my mission to try to help Uncle Sam retrieve the Pillars of Truth from Hell. So here I am.

HADES:

That presents an interesting dilemma. It is troublesome that you were beseeched. That is serious, especially if you are not sure why you were beseeched. If it does have something to do with the re- trieval of the Pillars of Truth, it could be a serious problem. For you see, it would appear as though your mission might well be the very same serious complication that I have on my hands at the present time. At present, those same Pillars of Truth are now here and I have no idea what to do with them. I can't just send them back, especially if they're not wanted back. They clearly don't belong here; yet they have been commanded to be here by the Trump Administration. As it turns out, Mr. Trump and his associates have no use for any of the Pillars of Truth and have sent them to Hell. What am I to do with them? As I said, they clearly don't belong here. It is obvious that they are no longer welcome in the United States so long as Donald Trump is President. It is apparent that I cannot hide them. They are far too radiant. This is a dark and dismal place. It is certainly no place for such lovely and flawless creatures. Just look behind you for they are all here. Did you mention that your guest Uncle Sam was here to find the Pillars of Truth? Well, here they are. Perhaps, Uncle Sam would like to visit with the Pillars of Truth before we set forth a plan for their return.

As Hades, Apollo, Dearth, and Uncle Sam turn they observe the Pillars of Truth lined up between where they are standing and the red colored rendition of "The White House" in the background. Hades walks to the left of the stage with Apollo following him while Dearth and Uncle Sam wander to the right of the stage while assessing the eight Pillars of Truth who are standing in groupings of two, three, and three. Spotlights are trained onto the eight elegant and statuesque Pillars in their radiant white robes. They each smile as Hades pounds his scepter and clears his throat to speak.

HADES:

It is important that I have undivided attention. The Pillars of Truth have been improperly sent to Hell and, at present, I have no place for them; yet, I cannot send them back to where they are unwanted and not welcome. Here, on a mission, is my nephew, Apollo, his acquaintance, Dearth, and the well know personage from the United States, Uncle Sam. It appears as though their mission is to seek the return of the Pillars of Truth to the United States. However, without some authority, other than the blank command by Apollo, there seems to be no basis for my releasing the Pillars of Truth. Accordingly, it is necessary for me to find a reason and the proper authority for a release of the Pillars.

APOLLO:

Perhaps, a mandate from the citizens from where they came.

HADES:

That may well be the key – a mandate. Perhaps if there were a mandate for their return, I might send them back. Otherwise, they must remain indefinitely at a place where they do not belong. Therefore, I will now allow Uncle Sam to go forward to speak to each of the Pillars about their return to the United States. After he has done so, it is my request that each of the Pillars stand before us to present the circumstances that forced each of them to Hell. Uncle Sam, would you be kind enough to speak with each of the Pillars to see if they wish to return to the United States?

It is at this stage that Uncle Sam walks over to the center right of the stage near where the Pillars of Truth are standing. He addresses each one as he walks along the line they form.

UNCLE SAM:

Tell me Ethics, is it your desire to return to you proper place in the U.S.?

ETHICS:

Yes. That is my desire. I wish to return to the U.S.

UNCLE SAM:

Tell me Integrity, is it your desire to return to you proper place in the U.S.?

INTEGRITY:

Yes. That is my desire. I wish to return to the U.S.

UNCLE SAM:

Tell me Honesty, is it your desire to return to you proper place in the U.S.?

HONESTY:

Yes. That is my desire. I wish to return to the U.S.

UNCLE SAM:

Tell me Loyalty, is it your desire to return to you proper place in the U.S.?

LOYALTY:

Yes. That is my desire. I wish to return to the U.S.

UNCLE SAM:

Tell me Courtesy, is it your desire to return to you proper place in the U.S.?

33333

333

33333

33333

3333

33333

3333

3333

333

333

COURTESY:

Yes. That is my desire. I wish to return to the U.S.

UNCLE SAM:

Tell me Reverence, is it your desire to return to you proper place in the U.S.?

REVERENCE:

Yes. That is my desire. I wish to return to the U.S.

UNCLE SAM:

Tell me Honor, is it your desire to return to you proper place in the U.S.?

HONOR:

Yes. That is my desire. I wish to return to the U.S.

UNCLE SAM:

Tell me Justice, is it your desire to return to you proper place in the U.S.?

JUSTICE:

Yes. That is my desire. I wish to return to the U.S.

Uncle Sam takes a position to the right of the Pillars of Truth and nods to Hades.

HADES:

Very well. That being the case, I want each of the Pillars of Truth to tell us why each of them should be released. Despite the fact that I operate the Underworld as I see fit, I intend to be completely fair. Therefore, it will be permitted for each of the Pillars of Truth to explain what caused them to be here. So that Mr. Trump can have his view expressed, I will allow us to enter into his subconscious in order for him to provide his side of the story. This will enable him to consciously continue with his current activities while we tap into his subconscious for his explanation as to why each of the Pillars of Truth was sent here.

Let us begin with Ethics, who stands nearest to me. Ethics, please explain yourself to us; tell us why you have come to be here; inform us as to why you should be released; and, finally, tell us where you expect to go.

Ethics steps forward. A radiant white beam shines upon her, while her purple sash seems amplified with an intense purple light. She steps forward from where she was standing next to Integrity. She clears her voice and states the reasons why she is in Hell, and why she should be released.

ETHICS:

I was sent to Hell by President Trump. He stated that he had no use for Ethics. He disregarded the ethical considerations relative to him continuing to own and attempt to operate his business interests while he is a sitting president. These actions are considered unethical. Issues arose relative to whether business partners were paying fair market value and whether certain people were the proper people with whom the President should do business.

It became apparent that many business associates to the President and his businesses were trying to gain political favor. Many of these people were of questionable character. Their relationship with the President of the United States is also considered to be unethical. Many of the business transactions that involved them and Mr. Trump were improper and could ultimately embarrass the United States. In some cases, the actual business partners remain anonymous and there is no way of knowing if some of those partners are adversaries of the United States or work against the interests of the United States. There are even business deals in Uruguay, India, Canada, Indonesia, and Dubai that are foreign deals that would typically be prohibited. Even though President Trump said that he is not involved in these business transactions, his family members have admitted that such is not the case. Recently, he asked the United States Ambassador to the United Kingdom to move the British Open Golf Tournament to a golf resort owned by Mr. Trump in Scotland. That is not only unethical but illegal.

Hades holds up his free hand to stop Ethics. He then points to the smoldering fire to the left of the stage where a spotlight focuses on Donald Trump, who appears as a cameo standing behind the smoldering fire in an open space between flames that shoot up on each side of the image of Donald Trump.

DONALD TRUMP:

Where am I? Is this a dream. I thought that I was doing a rally. Who are you? Who are these people?

HADES:

I am Hades. You are in Hell. Actually, and more precisely, it's your subconscious that is in Hell. Your conscious mind is conducting a rally and will not be disturbed. I have tapped into your subconscious mind in order to allow you to explain why you have sent each of the Pillars of Truth to Hell. Ethics, who stands next to me was just explaining what caused her to be sent to Hell by you. Did you hear what she said?

DONALD TRUMP:

I did hear her. Boy, I don't remember her looking that good. She's a real babe isn't she. I should have paid closer attention before I sent her to Hell.

HADES:

Please focus on what she said about your business dealings and the disregard you had for ethical requirements and the fact that you had some questionable business partners.

DONALD TRUMP:

My business is my business and who I do business with is not of Ethic's concern. I told her that and that I don't give two hoots about any ethics. Never did and never will. Boy, she is quite attractive.

HADES:

Stay focused on the issue. Can you offer any justification for you're not following ethical requirements?

DONALD TRUMP:

I don't need to since I'm the President. Is that all you got? If she agrees to forget about ethics she can come back. I always like to have attractive people around.

UNCLE SAM:

Wait! That's typical of Donald Trump. Plus, I'm sure that Ethics has more to say. Ethics, didn't President Trump say he would donate his salary, however, it does appear as though many, if not all, of those donations are supposedly for entities that do not exist. Plus, aren't his donations currently impossible to track. Didn't he promised to disclose his taxes; but has never done so and, in fact, has refused to do so.

ETHICS:

Yes. That was considered to be totally unethical. I tried to get Mr. Trump to do what all other presidents had done. However, he refused. I did try. In my defense, I tried to get President Trump to make proper disclosures, and to release his tax returns. I reminded him of the ethical considerations and that he had not acted in a proper or ethical manner. I asked him to change his ways and act ethically. He told me that he didn't need to be told about following any ethical rules or considerations. When I repeatedly insisted that he act ethically, he told me to go to Hell. Here I am. I don't want to be here. I want to go back to the United States where I belong. I feel that if I went back without some mandate, as you mentioned, or order from a high authority, he would send me straight back to Hell. I implore you to find a way for me to go back to the country I love. Please find a way for Ethics to return to the United States.

HADES:

Mr. Trump, do you have anything more to say about Ethics, or any response to what she just said?

DONALD TRUMP:

She's just making a mountain out of a mole hill. As I said, I can do what I want as long as I'm President. That's my position and I'm sticking to it.

HADES:

Although I have the authority to send Ethics back and even my nephew, Apollo, has the authority to see that Ethics goes back, judging from what Mr. Trump has said, there is no assurance that he will not send you right back to Hell again. Such a circular set of events would serve no purpose. Ethics would be shredded over and over again, perhaps until there was no meaning left for ethics. There must be found a mandate of some sort. Perhaps a voter mandate; or a Congressional mandate such as a conviction as a result of Articles of Impeachment. A mandate is needed. A mandate is essential. While you step back, let us think more about your situation Ethics. Meanwhile, let us turn our attention to Integrity. Please step forward Integrity. Kindly, explain yourself to us; tell us why you have come to be here; inform us as to why you should be released; and, finally, tell us where you expect to go.

Ethics steps back while Integrity steps forward. As she does, a radiant white beam shines upon her, while her green sash seems amplified with an intense deep green light. Integrity composes herself, clears her throat and speaks.

INTEGRITY:

My story is similar to that of Ethics. I purposely went to Mr. Trump to caution him that his actions were lacking in integrity and that he should change his ways. I even approached him during the campaign. I told him that he was saying one thing one time and then another thing later. He denied that he did that, so I pointed out specific instances where he had said something specific and then change it completely. He would respond either that he hadn't said the things I brought to his attention or that he had been misquoted. I told him that not only did I remember what he said but so did the media and the public. He called us all liars and said that the media was fake news.

HADES:

Mr. Trump, do you have any response to what Integrity has said about you?

DONALD TRUMP:

I don't remember her being so tall. I like tall ladies. I wonder how tall she is.

HADES:

Please stay focused on what Integrity said. She basically called you a liar and claims that you have no integrity. What do you have to say to that accusation?

DONALD TRUMP:

Everybody lies. Plus, the media and my political enemies are always misquoting me. Boy, she is tall. As I said, I like tall ladies.

UNCLE SAM:

Permit me to interrupt. First of all, Mr. Trump, would you please stay on subject. Now, Integrity, in regard to a couple of specific examples of Mr. Trump changing what he said, didn't he say before becoming President that Julian Assange and Wikileaks were traitors and should be shot; while later, and after becoming President, didn't he say that Assange and Wikileaks were bearers of the truth, which was certainly not the case. Also, and after the campaign, didn't Mr. Trump deny that the Russian hacks occurred or that Putin had helped him; when every one of the intelligence agencies had proof that the Russians and Putin had helped Trump.

INTEGRITY:

That's absolutely true. It also appeared as though Mr. Trump intended to profit from the presidency. I told him that it was improper for him to profit from the presidency. I also told him that he should not act or speak like a racist or to dig up dirt on a political opponent. I mentioned Hillary Clinton's emails that he begged the Russians to find. I pointed out the fact that he sided with discredited Ukrainian politicians regarding matters involving the Biden family. Then when the U.S. House of Representatives produced witness after witness and document after document regarding the misuse of presidential power to force the Ukraine into a compromising position by abusing the power of the presidency, I again implored President Trump to show some integrity and be truthful. Mr. Trump told me that I could go to Hell and that he didn't have a need for integrity.

Then, I reminded him of his lies about being wealthy, his failure to release tax returns, his escapades with a porn star and a *Playboy* model, the money he's gotten from Republican politicians and the campaign committee, and the many other abuses showing a lack of integrity. That was apparently it, for the next I realized it, I had been sent to Hell. No offense Mr. Hades, but I don't like it here. I want to be back in the United States. That's where I belong. Please find a way to send me back.

HADES:

Mr. Trump, I will give you another opportunity to defend yourself. How do you answer the accusations placed before us by Integrity?

DONALD TRUMP:

You know they're all quite tall. They could all come back and work for me if they agree to do what I say and give me complete loyalty.

HADES:

Those comments are rejected. Since Mr. Trump can't seem to stay on point, I see no reason for me to give him another chance to explain. Therefore, Integrity, let me tell you the same thing that I told Ethics. I have the authority to send you back and so does my nephew, Apollo. However, there is no assurance that President Trump will not send you right back to Hell again. Such a circular set of events would serve no purpose. Integrity would be shredded over and over. That would not be a good situation for you; nor would it be a good situation for anyone who valued Integrity. As I told Ethics, there must be found a mandate of some sort. Perhaps a voter mandate; or a Congressional mandate such as a conviction as a result of Articles of Impeachment. For that, there would need to be another impeachment process. In any event some sort of mandate is needed. A mandate is essential. At this time, I would like to have you step back while we think more about your situation Integrity. Meanwhile, let us turn our attention to Honesty. Please step forward Honesty. Please explain yourself to us; tell us why you have come to be here; inform us as to why you should be released; and, finally, tell us where you expect to go.

Integrity steps back while Honesty steps forward. As she does, a radiant white beam shines upon her, while her Ultra White sash seems amplified with an intensely bright light. Honesty composes herself, clears her throat and speaks while Donald Trump folds his arms in front of his chest and pouts.

HONESTY:

Thank you, Mr. Hades. I believe that my issues are a bit more involved than the issues faced by Integrity and Ethics. To start with, even though Mr. Trump has a supposed following of about 35 percent of the people in the United States, only 25 percent even believe him while 64 percent consider him to be a liar. So, even though a significant number of the people believe him to be a liar, he still manages to have a following that baffles my mind.

His total disregard for Honesty has me in total shame. I've never been this way before. I know that other Presidents have stretched the truth from time to time but never before has there been such a disrespect for Honesty. I was always able to "get by" with the fibs of other Presidents; however, with Mr. Trump there has been the most terrible relationship imaginable. He has a total disregard for me and has repeatedly told me to go to Hell. It is so bad that one major publication in the United States has catalogued over 16,200 false or misleading claims. I call them lies. This is evidence that there is no respect for Honesty. As a part of a certain media re-cordation process, it was reported that there were 492 false claims by Mr. Trump in his first 100 days in office. In 2017 the same publisher reported 1,999 false claims, while in 2018 they recorded an additional 5,689 false claims, and in 2019 they reported at least

8,155 suspected false statements by Mr. Trump. Clearly this is a blatant disrespect for Honesty.

He's gotten worse and worse. I have been beside myself. My name is in total disrepute due to the lies presented by Mr. Trump. There is no way anyone can keep up. He has shown a total disregard for me and for the truth. To be more specific, I told him that his claim that the trade agreements involving Canada and Japan were totally wrong regarding tariffs being eliminated. He said it was a $40 Billion deal and that was blatantly false. His statements about the United Nations, NATO, the TPP, NAFTA, the Paris Environmental Accord have all been totally dishonest.

HADES:

Mr. Trump, do you have any response to what Honesty has said about you?

DONALD TRUMP:

She reminds me of someone I knew in college. Ask her if she went to college in Philadelphia. See really does look familiar. I'm pretty sure that I have seen her somewhere before. Ask her if she's been to Philadelphia.

HADES:

No, I'm not going to ask her if she went to college in Philadelphia. How do you respond to her accusations about your lying?

DONALD TRUMP:

So, what if I lie about somethings? Everybody does. I like to do that to see if people really know what I talk about or if they just will agree with me. Most of my life, people just agree with me instead of contesting what I say. I've found that when I intimidate people, I can say about anything and they don't do anything about it.

UNCLE SAM:

That's the sort of what I would expect from you Donald. But, if Hades permits, I would like to hear more from Honesty. Perhaps she can tell us about your statements about Ukraine, and your comments regarding the impeachment? Those were not true either, where they? Or what about the claim that the United States economy is the best in history when it is actually one of the worst. In fact, the U.S. economy, at present, is nothing like it was under the presidential terms of Eisenhower, Johnson, Clinton or Obama. Isn't it true that during the Trump Presidency, the economy is probably about as bad, or worse, than it was during the Great Depression?

HONESTY:

You are correct. You're right about Ukraine and you are right about the impeachment. Plus, the economy under Mr. Trump is probably the worst in the history of the United States. Also, the tax cut that he falsely claims is the best in U.S. history is actually the eighth largest in 100 years. It's nowhere near the largest. He has stated that the United States has lost money on trade deficits which is totally false since with a basic understanding of economics, everyone knows that countries do not lose money on trade deficits.

Worse than that are his constant twitter misstatements. He has no shame. He actually seems to pride himself on being dishonest. I've told him in the sake of Honesty to please stop. So, he lost it with me and told me to go to Hell. So here I am. I don't want to be here. Please send me back.

HADES:

I believe that I've heard enough about Mr. Trump's lack of honesty. Therefore, Honesty, let me tell you the same thing that I told Ethics and Integrity. I have the authority to send you back and so does my nephew, Apollo. However, there is no assurance that President Trump will not send you right back to Hell again. There is absolutely no chance that Honesty can be preserved so long as Donald Trump is President. As mentioned to both Ethics and Integrity, there will need to be a mandate to rid the United States of the Trump Presidency in order for there to be a way for Honesty to return to the people of the country. Who knows if the elected officials would have the courage, fortitude, and, most particularly, the honesty to proceed with evidence of impeachment after which a conviction would result? Otherwise, it will take a mandate at the election booth. Other than such a mandate, I see no way that Honesty can return to the United States of America. Therefore, would you please step back while we think more about your situation Honesty. Now, let us turn our attention to Loyalty. Please come forward Loyalty. Please explain yourself to us; tell us why you have come to be here; inform us as to why you wish to return; and, finally, tell us where you expect to go.

Honesty steps back while Loyalty steps forward. As she does, a beautiful pink beam shines upon her, while her Pink sash seems amplified with an intensely bright light. Loyalty composes herself, clears her throat and speaks.

LOYALTY:

Thank you, Mr. Hades. Sorry, but I do not want to be here. Unfortunately, I have no choice. President Trump has repeatedly said that there is no place in the United States for Loyalty, unless it is undivided loyalty to him. From the time before Mr. Trump took office he stated, "I need loyalty, I expect loyalty." It turns out that he meant to him and not from him to the country or to any one or principle. Mr. Trump even stated that he valued "…loyalty above everything else – more than brains, more than drive and more than energy." So long as that loyalty was to him, nothing could have been truer. But he has no loyalty to others.

Initially, I had the misconception that when he spoke of Loyalty, he meant loyalty to the country, or to the Constitution, or to the principles of truth. Because of my misconception, I thought that Mr. Trump and I would get along famously. Then I realized that in Mr. Trump's mind, loyalty was a one-way street and didn't begin with a capital "L." The fact of the matter is that Mr. Trump expects his Cabinet, his aides, members of Congress, his supporters, and even Loyalty herself to lavish praise and total homage to him. I could not accept that. After all, I am Loyalty. So, I asked myself, "how could Loyalty, herself, lavish praise upon Mr. Trump." It was and is an impossible task. As I said, with Mr. Trump, it is not a situation of actual loyalty to one's country, or to principles, or the Constitution; but to show uncompromised loyalty to Donald Trump only.

HADES:

Mr. Trump? How do you respond to what Loyalty has stated about you? Is it true that you demand undivided loyalty form others but do not bother to show any loyalty in return either to others or to the Constitution?

DONALD TRUMP:

You know? She really looks good with that pink sash. Actually, I like all of the sashes; however, pink is especially becoming. I think that ladies look so good in pink. Wouldn't you agree?

HADES:

For heaven sakes Mr. Trump. Can't you stay on subject. This is getting very tiresome.

UNCLE SAM:

After studying and contemplating the situation, I surmised that this serious character flaw that Mr. Trump demonstrates constitutes inherent psychological and behavioral disorders that likely originated during a spoiled childhood of too many concessions by those who were around him in his youth. It is evident that no other President of the United States has had such a psychological deficiency. For example, and in my opinion, from perhaps the most loyal to the United States, George Washington and Abraham Lincoln, to the least loyal to the United States, Warren Harding and Andrew Jackson, no other President has lacked at least some loyalty to the country, the Constitution, and to the citizens. Mr. Trump has no such loyalty. His self-centered and ego-centric personality does not allow any space for any form of loyalty to others. Would you agree Loyalty?

LOYALTY:

I couldn't agree more. It is no wonder that at least twenty-seven of the most notable psychiatrists in the United States have questioned the mental health of Mr. Trump. Their consensus view is that Mr. Trump's mental state is a clear and present danger to the United States. That has proven to be true time after time. In regard to my own dealings with him, it became apparent that he has a total disregard for any loyalty to others. In such regard, he won't even recognize me or the concept I present for the country or its Constitution. Bluntly, there was no room in the United States for me and for him to coexist. When I confronted him about the Loyalty I represent to the United States, its Constitution, and its people, he summarily sent me to Hell. So, here I am wishing desperately to go back. I really don't belong here. Please send me back to the United States where Loyalty should stand for the relationship between all citizens, their country, the Constitution.

HADES:

Before I respond to that, I would like to hear from Mr. Trump. How do you respond to Loyalty.

DONALD TRUMP:

How is it that someone so attractive can be so nasty to me? I am sure that I am the best person Loyalty ever met. No one can come close to me. I deserve complete loyalty, especially since I am President. Most women are loyal to me because of my greatness and don't even need to be asked.

HADES:

Oh brother! Unfortunately, I must tell Loyalty the same thing that I told Ethics, Integrity, and Honesty. I have the authority to send you back and so does my nephew, Apollo. However, there is no assurance that President Trump will not send you right back to Hell again. There is absolutely no chance that Loyalty can be preserved for the citizens, the country, or its Constitution so long as Donald Trump is President. As mentioned to Ethics, Integrity, and Honesty, there will need to be a mandate to rid the United States of the Trump Presidency in order for there to be a way for Loyalty, as envisioned by citizens, the country and the Constitution, to return with balance. Now, let us turn our attention to Courtesy. Please come forward Courtesy. Please explain yourself to us; tell us why you have come to be here; inform us as to why you wish to return; and, finally, tell us where you expect to go.

Loyalty steps back while Courtesy steps forward. As she does, a radiant yellow beam shines upon her, while her Yellow sash seems amplified with an intensely bright light. Courtesy composes herself, clears her throat and speaks.

COURTESY:

As you know, I am called Courtesy, as well as, Comity, especially in government and international circles. It was a total surprise to me when I found myself on the way to Hell. I've led a proper life and have always treated everyone with respect and complete courtesy. Throughout my existence I've always expected that courtesy was something that was of mutual consideration between parties. Then I met Mr. Trump. With him, it was always a one-way street. He expected courtesy and respect form others; however, he has never demonstrated any courtesy or respect to anyone. In fact, he often makes up stories and lies about others in order to place them in a disrespectful position. He shows no courtesy whatever.

HADES:

Mr. Trump, how do you respond to what Courtesy has said?

DONALD TRUMP:

What? It didn't sound like anything important. Besides, I was just noticing how well the yellow sash went with her hair. That really looks good. It almost matches my hair.

HADES:

Didn't you hear what Courtesy said Mr. Trump?

DONALD TRUMP:

It was just some more boring stuff. This is getting a lot like the briefings that the Cabinet people and the Intelligence Officers do to waste my time.

UNCLE SAM:

If I may interrupt and correct me if I'm wrong; but what Mr. Trump does is called "projection" which is something that others would not consider. When psychologists use the term "projection" they pinpoint what one person, like Donald Trump, is aware of and what he might do in projecting a behavioral deficiency of others, which is really his own deficiency. What's more evident and astounding is the fact that Mr. Trump is incapable of showing any empathy. He is incapable of recognizing the pain of others who might be suffering because of an unforeseen medical situation, like COVID-19, or what the medical personnel are experiencing while caring for those sick individuals. Instead, he finds some sort of fault with others regardless of any unfortunate circumstances they may experience or any disability they may have or any misfortune that another person may experience.

COURTESY:

That would certainly be true from my perspective. At no time have I ever seen Mr. Trump demonstrate any form of courtesy to any other person. Instead, he is ready to insult or cast aspersions upon others as he did to every single one of his opponents during the presidential campaign, and as he repeatedly does with the members of the news media. He insults the media on a routine basis even though the media provides him millions of dollars-worth of free advertising time as he turns every press conference, meeting, bill signing, or other event into a political rally of free advertising. It doesn't end there. When the United States Congress passed the largest and most expensive spending bill in United States history, Mr. Trump insulted the Democrats who helped make it possible; instead of complimenting them as other presidents have done when an opposing party or an opposing individual has assisted in bringing about significant legislation or change for the citizens of our country.

What has been most frustrating to me has been the lack of courtesy that he has shown to military personnel and law enforcement personnel who have devoted their lives to the public while Mr. Trump had a bogus claim of bone spurs to keep him from any kind of service to his country. When I brought this fact to Mr. Trump's attention, he commanded me to go to Hell. That's when I lost it with him. His total disregard for women. His constant referring to women as "nasty" or "horrid" was fresh in my mind. So, I told him what I thought of him and his absolute lack of courtesy to anyone. He had me escorted out and told his associates to send me to Hell. Now, here I am. I definitely don't deserve to be here. There must be something that can be done. Courtesy belongs in the U.S.

HADES:

Mr. Trump? Do you care to add anything for your defense?

DONALD TRUMP:

I don't need to defend myself. I'm the President. Although, I will say that I do like a feisty woman, so long as she knows her place. This lady is feisty.

HADES:

That's enough. This situation keeps getting worse. Unfortunately, Courtesy, I must tell you the same thing that I told Ethics, Integrity, Honesty, and Loyalty. I have the authority to send you back and so does my nephew, Apollo. However, there is no assurance that President Trump will not send you right back to Hell again. There is absolutely no chance that Courtesy can be preserved for the citizens, the country, or its Constitution so long as Donald Trump is President. As mentioned to Ethics, Integrity, Honesty, and Loyalty, there will need to be a mandate to rid the United States of the Trump Presidency in order for there to be a way for Courtesy, as envisioned by citizens, the country and the Constitution, to return with balance. Now, let us turn our attention to Reverence. Please come forward Reverence. Please explain yourself to us; tell us why you have come to be here; inform us as to why you wish to return; and, finally, tell us where you expect to go.

Courtesy steps back while Reverence steps forward. As she does, a radiant beam shines upon her, while her Black sash seems to stand out as the intensely bright light reflects of her white gown. Reverence composes herself, and speaks while Donald Trump attempts to gesture a mocking imitation of Hades.

REVERENCE:

Please, your Eminence, believe me when I say that I am far more perplexed than any of my esteemed colleagues when I say that I do not belong here. Mr. Trump sent me, REVERENCE, of all people, to Hell. Imagine that! I asked myself how any individual who has throughout his life has shown a total disregard for the idea of reverence, can be the one to send me to Hell. From my view, Mr. Trump has never shown any respect or reverence for any other person during his entire lifetime. I realized that his former Energy Secretary, Rick Perry praised Mr. Trump as "God's chosen one;" while the president of Liberty University, Jerry Falwell Jr. considers Mr. Trump the evangelicals "dream president." Even Mr. Trump called himself the "Chosen One." These statements are completely baffling and no doubt blasphemy, as well. I also remember that Congressman Barry Loudermilk from Georgia compared Mr. Trump to Jesus Christ. Surely, that must be blasphemy. I am also aware that many white evangelicals approve of Mr. Trump regardless of his immorality, his thousands of lies, his deception, his adulterous conduct, his disrespect for those who are different or less fortunate, his rude behavior such as shoving another head of state out of the way so Mr. Trump could be in the front of a picture, and his general failure to follow what has been known throughout modern history as the basic morality of humanity.

HADES:

Mr. Trump? How do you respond to the allegations made about you by Reverence?

DONALD TRUMP:

I am the "Chosen One." Just ask a lot of the religious people who follow me. That's why I can do what I please. I don't need some sanctimonious lady to criticize me. Reverence should realize that her attitude takes away from her beauty. She should be humble, especially in my presence.

HADES:

Good Heavens! Mr. Trump, if you really believe that you are the "Chosen One," you will have a most incredible shock coming your way in the not too distant future. How did someone like you ever become President of the United States?

UNCLE SAM:

It was a fluke. In regard to Mr. Trump's Presidency, what Reverence said has certainly struck a chord with me. I asked myself: Is the world now upside down? Has the citizenry of the United States totally lost their moral compass by accepting such behavior by their president? Where does the matter of reverence now stand? What am I to do? Do you realize that on one occasion, Mr. Trump was asked if he asked God for forgiveness? He stated that he "… didn't think so…" and went on to say that if he thought he did something wrong he would try to make it right and not bring God into the picture. Then there is the disrespect that Mr. Trump has shown for the military and medical personnel. When he insulted the bereaved parents of a soldier who was killed in Iraq, that was too much. I can feel your frustration, Reverence.

REVERENCE:

Not only does the lack of the misplaced reverence by Mr. Trump and his disrespect for our country that concerns me; but so, does his outright contempt for world leaders and the multilateral global organizations that the United States has cultivated for decades in order to assure world peace and relationships. Mr. Trump's rude treatment of allies along with his disregard for NATO, the U.N., the Pacific Trade Agreement, his distortion and undermining of NAFTA, and his wanton disregard for the Paris environmental accord have all contributed to a total lack of reverence to what the United States has done as a world leader. The failure of Mr. Trump to demonstrate any form of leadership for the COVID-19 virus that has gripped the world is a further demonstration of his lack of reverence for mankind. Then, his mistreatment of medical workers and emergency personnel has been totally disrespectful along with a lack of reverence for those who daily try to help their fellow man. His attitude has been divisive and has fueled the wrong kind of nationalism across the globe. Then to top it off, he told me to go to Hell. Please, Mr. Hades, intervene as soon as possible. Mr. Trump has to be brought into check and made accountable for what he has done and what he is doing. It is a desperate and irreverent situation. Please help!

HADES:

Good heavens! This situation involving Mr. Trump keeps getting worse and worse. There is no need for Mr. Trump to provide any further response to you, Reverence. Of course, I want to do something for you. However, I must tell you the same thing that I told

Ethics, Integrity, Honesty, Loyalty, and Courtesy. I have the authority to send you back and so does my nephew, Apollo. However, there is no assurance that President Trump will not send you right back to Hell again. There is absolutely no chance that Reverence can be preserved for the citizens, the country, or its Constitution so long as Donald Trump is President. As mentioned to Ethics, Integrity, Honesty, Loyalty, and Courtesy, there will need to be a mandate to rid the United States of the Trump Presidency in order for there to be a way for Reverence, as envisioned by citizens, the country and the Constitution, to return with balance. Now, let me turn my attention to Honor. Please come forward Honor. Please explain yourself to us; tell us why you have come to be here; inform us as to why you wish to return; and, finally, tell us where you expect to go.

Reverence steps back while Honor steps forward. As she does, a radiant beam shines upon her, while her Blue sash seems to stand out as the intensely bright light reflects off her white gown. Honor composes herself, and speaks.

HONOR:

With all due respect Mr. Hades, I do not belong here. Pursuant to my namesake, I have led an honorable existence. The problem that I have had is that I always treat others with honor and respect; and as a result, there are those who take advantage of me. A major series of problems began for me when Donald Trump became the forty-fifth president of the United States. Up until that time, there were always some issues about a slip-up by a president in terms of being completely honorable. However, with Mr. Trump, his dishonesty, and constant lying drove me completely out of my element. In the case of Mr. Trump, his actions from day one have been totally dishonorable. Since he has been in office, I have been unable to find any honorable act to which I could relate. He has brought shame to me and to the United States of America.

Certainly, there have been moments of shameful activity by the financially well-endowed and there have been incidents where the country was embarrassed because of the actions of individuals in leadership roles. However, Mr. Trump has promoted a total culture of corruption, greed, dishonesty, lies, and self-aggrandizement. Mr. Trump will not heed or listen to his top security advisors; he will not follow the recommendations of leading diplomats; he will not acknowledge the vast knowledge that long term military leadership offers; he will not follow long standing and proper protocol; he will not listen to individuals who have served the United States for decades; he refuses to divest himself of business interests, particularly those that present a clear conflict of interest; and he will make no effort to follow the Constitution of the United States.

HADES:

Mr. Trump? Are you paying attention? What do you have to say to the accusations made regarding Honor?

DONALD TRUMP:

As I told you a while ago, this entire process is getting very boring. How do you expect me to pay attention to all the boring talk about what others think? What's important is what I think and I am the President. That's what's important. Here is another beautiful creature who diminishes her natural beauty by saying a bunch of boring and disrespectful things about me.

HADES:

Apparently, Mr. Trump has nothing to contribute to this discussion. Anything more from Honor or Uncle Sam?

UNCLE SAM:

I'd like to ask Honor to clarify what happened when she brought these matters regarding the conflicts of interest and the improper business dealings to the attention of Mr. Trump relative to the Emoluments Clause of the Constitution?

HONOR:

When I brought these matters to the attention of Mr. Trump, he told me that he didn't care about the Emoluments Clause nor did he care about honor. He chastised me as being too sensitive and too careful. He told me that lying was what was behind his success and that was the way the world is today. I protested and stated that was not the case and that there was still honor in the world and in the United States. He said that I had been spending too much time listening to fake news. He then insisted that the way forward was to "…never give a sucker an even break. It is dog eat dog. You should take advantage of everyone else before they attempt to take advantage of you." Again, I protested and insisted that he attempt to act honorably.

Finally, I reminded him of the long list of his political associates who are either in jail or on their way to jail. I also mentioned the fact that he has had so many cabinet members that were or are under the cloud of scandals. He then claimed that they were either losers or they were wrongfully convicted or they were too reckless; so, they got caught. I tried to remind him that Honor was really a guardrail against the undermining of morality and without Honor the United States would become a third world enterprise. It was at that point where he came violently angry with me. He lost any semblance of dignity or honor and told me to go straight to Hell. I don't want to be here and I am confident that I should not be here. An articulate writer by the name of Marshall Helmberger of the publication known as _Timberjay_, once wrote in an article entitled *"Whatever happened to honor and integrity in America?"*:

"When we say that it's fine for the leader of the country to lie multiple times a day, to bully the less powerful, to dishonor the dead, to pal around with criminals, white supremacists, and dictators, and to pay hush money to porn stars, we can no longer claim any kind of moral high ground. We can no longer pretend that morality or decency or honor has a place in American society. When we don't speak out in opposition to the debasement that President Trump's actions represent to this country and its sense of identity, we dishonor ourselves. When an entire political party is willing to prostrate itself before such a man, it has lost any claim to legitimacy it might have once had."

I could not articulate the point more specifically or better. So, I referenced this matter to Mr. Trump. Again, he went into a rage and told me to stop paying attention to fake news. I protested and he told me to go straight to Hell. Here I am. I want to go back where I belong but I don't know how to get back. Can you help me?

HADES:

I am so sorry to hear this. All of the reports that you and the other Pillars of Truth have provided to me are indeed perplexing. I do want to help you and I do believe that something must be done. However, I must tell you the same thing that I told Ethics, Integrity,

Honesty, Loyalty, Courtesy, and Reverence. I have the authority to
send you back and so does my nephew, Apollo. However, there is
no assurance that President Trump will not send you right back
to Hell again. There is absolutely no chance that Honor can be
preserved for the citizens, the country, or its Constitution so long
as Donald Trump is President. As mentioned to Ethics, Integrity,
Honesty, Loyalty, Courtesy, and Reverence there will need to be
a mandate to rid the United States of the Trump Presidency in
order for there to be a way for Honor, as envisioned by citizens,
the country and the Constitution, to return with balance. Now,
let me turn my attention to Justice. Please come forward Justice.
Please explain yourself to us; tell us why you have come to be here;
inform us as to why you wish to return; and, finally, tell us where
you expect to go.

*Honor steps back while Justice steps forward. As she does, a radiant
beam shines upon her, while her Silver sash seems to stand out as the
intensely bright light reflects off her white gown. Justice composes
herself, and speaks. Trump throws his hands in the air and turns
his back to the proceedings.*

JUSTICE:

May what I have to say please your eminence. As Justice, I have
always had a special role when it comes to democracy. More particularly, my role as a member of the Pillars of Truth has been to
provide assurance that the United States does not slip into tyranny; for it has long been said that the judicial system is the final
bulwark against tyranny. As is well known, Justice is the founda-
tion of any judicial system. In the United States, special heed and
reference has been placed upon the importance of Justice as it is
recognized as the cornerstone of a democratic state throughout
the Constitution and laws of the country. I am proud that I have

carried that banner successfully throughout nearly 250 years of government in the United States. Certainly, there have been instances where individuals holding the base of power in the country have attempted to deviate from Justice and the Pillars of Truth. Ultimately those individuals were either brought to justice or themselves recognized their deviation from Justice and resigned.

However, in the case of Donald Trump there is an individual who has no concept of Justice; nor does he recognize the Pillars of Truth. I have determined that he is either too ignorant or too self-centered to even understand the concept of truth and justice. Never in the history of the United States has there been a person so oblivious to truth and justice. Never in the history of the United States has there been a public official who was such a prolific liar. Never in the history of the United States has there been a public servant who deviated from truth and justice in order to serve only himself and his self-interests. Because of these facts, I decided to confront Mr. Trump directly.

HADES:

Mr. Trump? Were you able to hear what Justice had to say while your back was turned to her? Don't you think that was rude?

DONALD TRUMP:

It's not rude. That's the way I do business. If I hear something, I don't like I often turn my back or do something else or even walk out. And, I don't care how many attractive ladies you bring forward. You'd at least think that someone with the name Justice would at least have gray hair and lots of wrinkles.

HADES:

What about the accusations? Do you have any defense to what Justice has said? Are you so superficial that you concern yourself with only appearances instead of substance?

DONALD TRUMP:

Appearances mean a lot to me and that's important since I am President. Besides, the substance just amounts to a boring lecture. I'm tired of these lectures. All of these ladies owe me undivided allegiance and that's it. Period.

HADES:

Is there anything more from either Lady Justice of Uncle Sam?

UNCLE SAM:

Yes, please. If I may ask Justice, when you confronted Mr. Trump, did you give him your reasons? Did you tell him why it was important that he accept and recognize Justice? Did you remind him of the connection between Justice and Truth?

JUSTICE:

I certainly did. When I met with Mr. Trump, I bluntly told him that never before has there been a public official who undermined the Constitution, the rule of law and democracy as he has. I also told him that during the entire history of the United States there have never been actions so blatantly contrary to Justice than his efforts to undermine the Justice Department, the Intelligence Agencies, and the other government departments through his personal actions and his appointments of totally incompetent individuals to key positions. I challenged his assault on the judicial system and his personal attacks on members of the judiciary who have dedicated their lives to the Constitution and the rule of law. I even questioned his loyalty to the United States and wondered aloud in his presence whether he was a Russian operative.

He was obviously irritated with me. However, I wasn't done. I pushed on and told him that he has bent the judicial system in ways never imagined, especially his attempts to interfere with the Michael Flynn matter, the Roger stone matter, the Paul Manafort manner, his upending the outstanding and well-respected prosecutors across the country, his trashing of the diplomatic corps, his disregarding the intelligence agencies, and his general eroding of the United States long-standing reputation in supporting the rule of law. I reminded him that over 2,000 former members of the Justice Department have expressed concern about the way Justice has been undermined and have demanded the resignation of the Attorney General who has become known as "Black Barr."

It was at that point that Mr. Trump sent me to Hell. So here I am along with the other members of the Pillars of Truth. Please help us. It is important for the United States, its citizens, and, frankly, the citizens of the world for we Pillars of Truth to be sent back to the United States to see if we can attempt to regain our proper standing. Please help us now.

HADES:

This is certainly the last straw. Even here in Hell we administer justice. In fact, my job is to administer justice as I see fit. I have to admit that does present certain perverse pleasure. But, having the Pillars of Truth here in Hell has certainly not enhanced my ability to administer justice when Justice and, more particularly, the Pillars of Truth, have been forced out of the United States, a country that has historically stood for justice and for truth. Clearly, I must do something and so I will. However, my place is here. I cannot leave. Apollo, I find that it is necessary for me to place in your charge and the charge of Uncle Sam the Pillars of Truth and ask that you find a way to have them reinstated in their proper place in the United States of America. I know that you will agree with me, especially since you made it your mission to come here along with Uncle Sam, and, I guess, Dearth, in order to find the Pillars of Truth and return them. So, if you have a plan, as Dearth indicates, please fill me in. Meanwhile Mr. Trump, you may have your subconscious back. You are free to leave Hell for now. Be assured that I will see you later.

The subconscious of Donald Trump dissolves from between the flames at the right of the stage. Then, Apollo draws Hades aside to a private huddle. The two of them confer with Hades listening to Apollo. From time to time Hades nods approvingly and smiles a devilish sort of smile. Hades then turns to the audience and states:

HADES:

You, watchful people, will need to see what my creative nephew has in mind for the return of the Pillars of Truth. Please pay careful attention to his plan as it unfolds. I think you will like it.

ACT THREE

The scene is set at the White House only it no longer appears white. The White House now appears in a dark shade of grey and is lighted in shades of grey including streaks of dark grey. After the curtain rises and entering at the left of the stage is Apollo, along with Uncle Sam, Dearth, and the eight Pillars of Truth, who line up behind Apollo, Uncle Sam and Dearth, situating themselves in a line from the left of the stage to the left center of the stage.

To the far right of the stage are standing Fruity Rudy, Moscow Mitch, Bad Barr, The Fox, and Donald Trump. The five of them are in a low discussion. They look up to the left of the stage as Apollo and the others enter.

At the center front of the stage between the White (now grey) House and the front of the stage are twelve individuals, including: Joe Construct, a middle-aged construction worker; Dr. Althea Medic, an intelligent young doctor; Mr. Big Jeans, a seasoned and rugged

*farmer; Miss Lilith Ruler, a bright young elementary teacher;
Earnest Craft, a labor union member; Father Doubt, an elderly
man of the cloth; Wilber Reeve, a government employee; William
Four Seasons, a Native American Tribal Leader; Professor Probe,
a research scientist; Jane Blonde, a well-known intelligence officer;
Aphrodite Gaia, a maître d, and S.H. Consular, a life-long diplomat. The lighting is such that these twelve individuals cannot be
clearly seen but their images in the shadows are obvious.*

*Apollo, Uncle Sam, and Dearth, deliberately move from the left of
the stage to the left center of the stage half way between the White
House and the audience. They stop at the left center of the stage near
the Pillars of Truth. The Pillars of Truth situate themselves next
to the twelve new individuals at the center back of the stage. Mr.
Trump and his entourage move forward from their position at the
right of the stage away from the awning to a position at the center
right of the stage. The twelve individuals in the shadows standing
at the center back of the stage are positioned so they can each step
forward to the center of the stage and in the full light when called
forward.*

TRUMP:

What are you doing here Apollo? Also, why are Uncle Sam,
Dearth, and the Pillars of Truth here? I thought that I had sent all
of you to Hell. Didn't you listen to me? Now go away and get out
of my sight before you ruin the last part of my rally.

APOLLO:

We've all been to Hell and back. Perhaps you failed to realize
that you have no power over me. On the other hand, I have the
power to bring certain parties back from Hell; just as Alcestis

was brought back from Hell by Hercules when Alcestis died for her husband King Admetus while I satisfied the command of Zeus to live as a herdsman for King Admetus. If you, Mr. Trump, had read any of the many plays written about Alcestis, including that of Thornton Wilder's Play entitled *The Alcestiad*, you would know of such returns from Hell. But, of course, I realize that you choose not to read. It has been said that you may not have that ability, which is too bad. You are missing so much. If you read, your spelling might improve.

TRUMP:

I don't have to take your insults. I am the President. I am a brilliant person. I am one of the smartest people ever. In fact, I'm sure that I'm the smartest person to ever be President. You and all of those with you can go straight back to Hell as far as I'm concerned.

APOLLO:

You don't have that power and you didn't in the first place. Although you made an effort to send the Pillars of Truth and Uncle Sam to Hell, you simply don't have that kind of power. Although my coming here was an accident due to your poor tweet and grammar, now that I am here, I intend to rectify the situation. Besides, Hades has no place for the Pillars of Truth. I intend to begin the process of getting the Pillars of Truth and Uncle Sam back to where they belong. We have much to discuss and I have a plan to implement. I will now devote my attention to the people who are standing between us. I believe that I will want to speak to them. But first, please, tell me who they are and why they are here?

TRUMP:

They came for the rally that we just had. I have good rallies. People like my rallies. People like me. They know I am great. They know I am special.

APOLLO:

Oh, you're special alright. (A long pause while Apollo moves a bit closer to center stage) Now, let's see just how special you are. Since I expect a mandate and the voice of the citizens to be overwhelming for your removal from office, let's see just what you have done for the people and if there is any reason for them to continue to support you. I expect when they hear the truth, they will not want to support you or your administration. In fact, let's hear from them.

TRUMP:

You are so wrong. The people…you know…these people just love me. It's all love. They all love me. I am so popular that I could be their president forever.

APOLLO:

Well. Let's explore that matter. Before we came here, I asked Uncle Sam to randomly select twelve individuals to serve as a jury of your peers.

TRUMP:

That's fine with me. If Sam selected twelve people from my rally, he will find that those people all love me. They're not my peers.

In order for there to be peers of mine, they would all need to be billionaires.

APOLLO:

You surprise me. I didn't know that you had a sense of humor. You and billionaires being peers. That is funny. Not only from the standpoint that you are not really a billionaire but from the standpoint that in the United States of America one's peers are people who are randomly chosen and then selected from a jury pool. That in and of itself makes me quite proud.

TRUMP:

Why would the jury system of the United States make you proud? You don't even belong here. Why Just go back to Greece and leave? Or, better yet, why don't you go to Hell like I told you earlier.

APOLLO:

Let me enlighten you, if that is even possible. The selection of twelve individuals to serve as jurors actually finds its basis in Greek mythology. In a play called *Oresteia*, I saved Orestes from being executed by the Furies, a trio of goddesses who were considered the instruments of justice. The Furies wanted to kill Orestes for killing his mother, Clytemnestra, who had killed Orestes father, Agamemnon.

TRUMP:

Sounds like a good plan. I like revenge. I use it all the time. So do my attorneys. An eye for an eye.

APOLLO:

That is the old Hammurabi Code. It is not followed in the United States.

TRUMP:

It should be. It should be up to the President and his cabinet to decide.

APOLLO:

That is another example of how poorly read you are. In the United States there is a jury of one's peers who decide the fate of criminal acts. Your Founding Fathers deliberated long and hard on the system of justice to be used. They chose the system that was originally developed by the Greeks. In doing so, they actually ended up following what was first set forth from the *Oresteia,* as I mentioned. In that case, I was the one who saved Orestes from the Furies and ultimately prevailed upon the Goddess Athena for help whereupon she set up a trial by a jury of twelve individuals. In that case and due to a split between the jurors, she cast the ultimate and deciding vote to determine that Orestes would not be killed. The idea was to stop the endless cycle of revenge and, in its place, provide a civilized jury trial allowing for a court decision rather than to allow individuals to take revenge.

TRUMP:

I like revenge better. I use it all of the time. If people cross me, they end up paying the price. I like revenge. It is the American way.

APOLLO:

No, it is not the American way. If it were, and after you leave office, your fate would be sealed in a most egregious way. Be thankful that revenge is not the American way.

TRUMP:

We'll see. I may be in office forever. The people like me so much. If I wanted, the people would keep putting me back into office.

APOLLO:

That is not the case. It is against the Constitution and in a vote you'd lose.

TRUMP:

Well, let's just see. You said that Sam was going to select some people who attended the rally. If they were at my rally that's fine. They all love me.

APOLLO:

We will see about that. Uncle Sam have you selected twelve individuals at random from the rally?

UNCLE SAM:

I have. The twelve who I have selected stand behind you at this time.

APOLLO:

Excellent. Permit me to start with the first person, the gentleman in the yellow hard had and working clothes. You sir, would you please come forward and tell me who you are and why you are here.

Joe Construct steps forward from the shadows and faces Apollo at center stage. He gives a bow to Apollo, clears his throat and faces the audience. However, before he can speak, Trump, Fruity Rudy, Moscow Mitch, Bad Barr, and the FOX all try to interrupt by speaking all at once.

TRUMP:

I've changed my mind. I'll not have this. I want you to leave Apollo along with the Pillars of Truth, Uncle Sam, and Dearth. Leave now. Go to Hell.

FRUITY RUDY:

We can't have this. They need to go. They will ruin everything.

MOSCOW MITCH:

Why. Why. Why. Sir, we can't have any of this. Tell them to go. I say. Why, I say. What is the meaning of this? They must go. Definitely, must go.

BAD BARR:

This should not be permitted. This Administration has suspended the Constitution. They need to be escorted out. Now!

THE FOX:

Something will need to be printed about this rude interruption.
I will...

*While Trump, Fruity Rudy, Moscow Mitch, Bad Barr, and the Fox
are all trying to speak at once, Apollo raises his hand in the air and
swirls it around several times. When he finishes, Trump, Fruity
Rudy, Moscow Mitch, Bad Barr, and the FOX lips keep moving and
they continue to gesture as if they are still in animated conversation;
however, no sound is heard.*

APOLLO:

As you will see and experience, Mr. Trump, Fruity Rudy, Moscow
Mitch, Bad Barr, and the FOX, you may continue to speak and
gesture; however, because of what I have done to you, no sound
will be heard from any of you. Feel free to wear yourselves out and
continue to attempt to speak; however, no one will hear a word
you say until I allow it. As you might expect, I will not allow it
until I am good and ready. For at this point, I want to hear what
is really on the minds of the people who have attended your rally.
Now, we will hear from the first guest and juror. It is time for the
real voice of the people to be heard. The one other command that
I will issue is that each of these rally guests, and now jurors, *must*
tell the truth. I will command each of them to tell us who they
are; why they came to the rally; and what they each now honestly
think as a result of what has transpired during your presidency.
Let us start with you sir.

*Finally, and after much gesturing, Trump, Fruity Rudy, Moscow
Mitch, Bad Barr, and the FOX realize that no one can hear anything they are trying to say, so they all stop attempting to speak*

and decide to listen. Trump crosses his arms in front of him like a three-year-old. Fruity Rudy spins his eyes. Bad Barr puffs about. Moscow Mitch prances about like a chicken and the FOX turns his back to the proceedings.

JOE CONSTRUCT:

My name is Joe Construct and I have been a construction worker for over twenty years. I was invited to Mr. Trump's rally and was promised that if I came, I would be paid for my expenses. Plus, I expected to hear first-hand as to how President Trump was going to make America great again.

APOLLO:

Was America not great when Mr. Trump took over?

JOE CONSTRUCT:

Actually, it was always great. I guess that I just got caught up in the rhetoric and let my emotions run away with the mood. Plus, I have to admit that I was taken in by Mr. Trump's statements about other races. I felt that I had something in common with Mr. Trump since he was white like me and that white people had been forgotten in past administrations.

APOLLO:

Was that true? Had white people been forgotten in past administrations? As Apollo, I expect for you to tell me the truth.

JOE CONSTRUCT:

To be bluntly honest, no! In fact, and as I think about it...we workers weren't forgotten before Mr. Trump was elected. Actually, we've always had a bit of an advantage over other races. As I said, I just got caught up in what Mr. Trump was saying. I have to confess that I went along with the emotional pitch. If the truth be told, I do work with other individuals, who are of different races, and they're really not too bad. When I give it some thought, they're just like me trying to take care of themselves and their families. They have to put bread on the table just like I do. From listening to them they love their families and are just trying to make a good living for their spouses and kids in trying to provide a good home. Even our interests like sports and having some fun are similar. So, in facing you and expecting to tell the truth, the people I know with different skin colors and religious beliefs are pretty much just like me when it comes down to it.

APOLLO:

Tell me Mr. Construct, is America better now that Mr. Trump is President? Are you better off? Has America become great?

JOE CONSTRUCT:

Since I am facing your eminence and required to tell the truth. I must confess that America is not better now that Mr. Trump is President. Bluntly, I am not better off and America is not as great as it once was. Mr. Trump has been a real disappointment for all of us.

APOLLO:

Why is that? Can you be specific and give me some reasons why?

JOE CONSTRUCT:

First of all, my wages have not increased while it costs me more to live. I even took another job to make ends meet. I lost that second job when the Coronavirus hit. Now, I'm worried about my construction job. Never before in my lifetime has the unemployment been so high. When I think about it, employment was nearly at an all-time high when Mr. Trump took over. Now it's the unemployment rate that is high... between 10% and 15% which is the worse it has been since the Great Depression. Over 40,000,000 people have filed for unemployment. I'm worried that I might soon be part of that group. Honestly, I'm worse off now under Mr. Trump than I have ever been. I'm really concerned, especially since even Mr. Trumps Treasury Secretary, Steven Mnuchin said that unemployment could reach over 25%. I'm really concerned.

APOLLO:

In addition to what you just mentioned, is there anything that you can think of that would make you believe that you are better off with Mr. Trump?

JOE CONSTRUCT:

Now that I think about it, the answer is no. Mr. Trump has been President for nearly four years and some of the things he has done have actually worked against me. For example, the pay increase of 2.1 percent for government employees that had been passed during the Obama administration was cancelled by the Trump Administration; the overtime pay for workers by the Obama Administration was abandoned; the requirement of records for workplace injuries was scrapped; anti-labor people were appointed to the National Labor Relations Board by Mr. Trump;

the oversight for many laws have been gutted; the significance of labor unions has been undermined; and health care is harder to get and is more expensive. One of the greatest concerns I have is worker's safety and Mr. Trump has acted is many ways to undermine safety at the workplace.

APOLLO:

Based upon what you just told me, would you want to see Mr. Trump continue as President of the United States?

JOE CONSTRUCT:

After giving it considerable thought, there is no way that I would like to see Mr. Trump remain as President of the United States. I guess that when it is all said and done, I will vote against him.

APOLLO:

Mr. Trump, you look frustrated. Any comment?

TRUMP:

Brainwashing. You're brainwashing him. You're twisting his words. Fake words, a fake construction worker and a fake god. Fake, fake, fake!

APOLLO:

Thank you, Mr. Trump and thank you Mr. Construct. Now would the next person please step forward, state your name, and tell us who you are and why you are here.

As instructed, Joe Construct steps back a bit so that he is still seen in full light, while Dr. Althea Medic steps forward into the spot-light to address Apollo.

DR. ALTHEA MEDIC:

This is a real treat to meet you, Apollo. This is a special moment for me since I studied Greek Mythology in college. I am known as Dr. Althea Medic. It is my belief that I was predestined to be a doctor since my given name, Althea, which has a Greek origin, means 'to heal.' I have been a practicing doctor for fifteen years after completing my residency in Internal Medicine. Recently, I have been on special assignment for the treatment of the COVID-19 epidemic. I was invited to the rally at the White House. I decided to come since I had never seen the White House before.

APOLLO:

Where you a supporter of Mr. Trump for President and do you still support him after attending this rally?

DR. ALTHEA MEDIC:

When Mr. Trump first ran for office, I was taken in by his promise to improve medical care and medical coverage for the public. However, shortly after he took office, he started talking about getting rid of the Affordable Care Act. That was a concern of mine and most of the entire medical sector since the Affordable Care Act actually made it better for the payment of medical expenses. When Mr. Trump started to make changes to the Affordable Car Act, many of us protested in major cities, including Boston, Chicago, Madison, New York City, Philadelphia, and Seattle. It became apparent that the changes that Mr. Trump proposed were ultimately harmful to both the patients and those of us who are providers. Additionally, several medical organizations that represent over 400,000 physicians and medical students urged Congress to protect a patient's right and access to health care. In fact, now only about 15% of the medical profession support Mr. Trump and his efforts to eliminate the Affordable Health Care Act. What is extremely frightening is the fact that no one in the Trump Administration has either presented or proposed a solution for all of the individuals who would be without health care insurance if the ACA were to be abolished. I can no longer support him.

APOLLO:

If Mr. Trump and his administration were to come up with a plan to replace the ACA would you be satisfied and, if so, would you support Mr. Trump?

DR. ALTHEA MEDIC:

I'm afraid not. He has often stated that he has a plan for something but never does. In my view, he has no credibility. We medical professionals rely on the truth and we rely on science. Mr. Trump has repeatedly proven the fact that he cannot be believed and that he doesn't place any faith in science. A cornerstone of the medical profession is science. Nearly everything that we do in medicine has a scientific basis. Mr. Trump is so far afield when it comes to science, there are few people left in the medical sector who can support him. For generations the medical profession has supported Republicans; however, that is no longer the case and that is almost exclusively due to Mr. Trump.

UNCLE SAM:

Other than the two items that you have just mentioned, namely, the Affordable Care Act and science, is there any reason why you believe that the medical profession can no longer support Mr. Trump?

DR. ALTHEA MEDIC:

Certainly. To start with, Mr. Trump removed the principal deputy of the Inspector General of the Department of Health and Human Services after she issued a detailed report regarding testing and supply shortages in hospitals that were responding to the coronavirus pandemic. I believe that she was removed by Mr. Trump because she pointed out the severe shortages of testing supplies, inadequate staffing, and concerns over hospital capacities. Additionally, Mr. Trump proposed CDC budget cuts by 16% and a slash of $3 billion for global health programs at a time when more funds should be allocated. Also, Mr. Trump has failed to fill key positions at the National Security Council pandemic office or its director. He has downplayed the severity of the pandemic; he has spread false information about COVID-19; and he allowed the crises to unfold while he cut funds and personnel. The last straw was when he urged doctors to lie about the virus and its consequences. All of these acts have made it more problematic for those of us in the medical profession to do our jobs and keep people healthy.

APOLLO:

Based upon what you just told us, would you want to see Mr. Trump continue as President of the United States?

DR. ALTHEA MEDIC:

Absolutely not. Under no circumstances would want Mr. Trump remain as President of the United States. I will vote against him.

APOLLO:

What do you have to say in response Mr. Trump?

TRUMP:

Arrogance and stupidity. That's what it is. The Obama Care thing is just wrong. Nobody wants it. My plan is better. Just wait and see. I've got a great plan. It's the best medical plan ever.

APOLLO:

Would you tell us? What is it? How is it better?

TRUMP:

It's just better. Just wait and see. It's the best.

APOLLO:

Would you give us a hint about how your plan would work?

TRUMP:

Nope! I don't need to tell you anything. It will be better once I have time to think it out. I'll think of something and when I do, it will be the greatest. It will be better than any plan ever.

APOLLO:

Okay…well,…thank you Mr. Trump and thank you, Dr. Medic. Now would the next person please step forward, state your name, and tell us who you are and why you are here.

Dr. Medic steps back a bit so that she is standing next to Joe Construct and is still seen in full light. Mr. Big Jeans steps up to address Apollo.

MR. BIG JEANS:

My name is Big Jeans. I'm a farmer and I have long supported Mr. Trump. At least I did until recently. Many people, including Mr. Trump, take farmers and ranchers for granted because they are under the misconception that we are not well educated and that we are taken in by emotional pitch. Let me tell you that is far from the truth. Take me for example, I have an undergraduate degree in chemistry. I planned on being a veterinarian; however, I enjoyed chemistry so much that I got my PhD in Applied Chemistry and began work for a major pharmaceutical company that explored new medications for farm animals. When my father retired from farming, I took over the family farm. I've been farming for nearly thirty years and during that time I've see the ups and downs of farm income. What is disturbing to me is the fact that farm income is well off the high peak of 2013. That was probably one of my best years as a farmer. I have to admit that it was during the Obama Administration. I just thought that things would get better under Mr. Trump; but I was dead wrong.

APOLLO:

Why? Did you think things would improve under Mr. Trump?

BIG JEANS:

I did. However, the Trump trade deals have disrupted not only my farming operations but the operations of many of my farmer friends. In my opinion, Mr. Trump screwed up both the NAFTA arrangement and the Trans-Pacific Partnership. Sure, neither of those were perfect; however, they could have been refined instead of abandoned. So many of the markets, especially the foreign markets, that we farmers counted on were disrupted when Mr. Trump scrapped those agreements. The tariffs, especially the ones involving Canada and Mexico have hurt us badly; and the Chinese tariffs wiped out what was the biggest soybean market. Prices have gone to hell. When one considers the disruption caused by the loss of those two agreements along with the ending of the ethanol options that we had before Mr. Trump took over, I can no longer go along with promises that things will get better when it's all talk and no action. I am more fortunate than others since I haven't had to consider bankruptcy; however, I have many friends in the farming business who have had to declare. Recently, I read that farm bankruptcy filings have jumped 20%, which is the highest level since 2011. The suicide level is high.

APOLLO:

Did farm profitability change? Didn't Mr. Trump provide subsidies?

BIG JEANS:

He did but that's not the point. We farmers measure our profitability by our net income. When our operating profit margin drops under ten percent we are in trouble. We can't make it. Today many of the average farmers have to take outside jobs in order to make ends meet. For me personally, I am lucky since I am in the top five percent of farmers. But even as one of the big farmers, who receive the most when it comes to farm payment programs, I am running my farm at a near cost basis. If it gets much worse, I'll be in trouble and, as I said, I am in the top five percent. If it had not been for the $28 Billion in farm subsidies, my farming operation would not have been above water. People are fast to criticize the farm subsidies; however, if we hadn't had them, the entire farming industry would have been in trouble. We needed the subsidies since the sales of farm goods experienced a 50% drop between 2018 and 2019. Both of those years were Trump years and a significant drop from the high of 2012. Just considering China alone, the U.S. sold about $26 Billion in 2012 but only about $9.1 Billion in 2018. The promised subsidies from the Trump Administration don't even come close to what the market was before he messed around with NAFTA and TPP. The $22.4 Billion in subsidies didn't off-set the market that was once established under the Obama Administration. Besides, we farmers don't want subsidies, we want a fair price for what we produce.

APOLLO:

Are you prepared to support Mr. Trump as you have in the past? Or not.

BIG JEANS:

Not. I will no longer support Mr. Trump. In good conscience, I cannot find any way to support him. He has ended our biofuel options. He sold us out to his friends in the oil industry. He has ruined our trade with other countries. This will continue or get even worse so long as we have a trade war going with China. Mr. Trump has constantly lied to the farmers and until now, we kept giving him the benefit of the doubt. We continued to support him. But, no longer. We'll no longer accept the lying.

APOLLO:

Mr. Trump. How do you respond to Mr. Big Jeans?

TRUMP:

How ungrateful. I give you farmers all of this money. I'm the best friend a farmer ever had. I give lots of money to farmers. The farmers never had it so good. No other President has done as much for farmers as I have. What do I get in return? A farmer who will say anything to be on the good side of somebody who claims to be a god. What lack of gratitude. It's disgusting. You're not a real farmer.

APOLLO:

Thank you, Mr. Trump and thank you Mr. Big Jeans. Let consider the record and let the real facts, and not alternative facts, speak for themselves. Now would the next person please step forward, state your name, and tell us who you are and why you are here.

At this point, Mr. Big Jeans steps back a bit so that he is standing next to Dr. Medic but still seen in full light. Miss Ruler steps up to address Apollo.

MISS RULER:

As you wish Lord Apollo. My name is Lilith Ruler and I am an elementary school teacher. Three years ago, I was a supporter of Mr. Trump for President of the United States. While he's been President, especially during the COVID-19 crises, I developed some misgivings about whether I would continue to support him. For that reason, I came to the rally. I needed to see for myself if Mr. Trump was softening his position about education and the teaching profession. I must say that I am quite disappointed.

APOLLO:

Tell me why are you disappointed?

MISS RULER:

Since Mr. Trump has been in office and since Betsy DeVos has been in charge of education, there has been one disappointment after another. The funding for education has declined sharply resulting in teachers walking out of their classrooms across the country, and that particularly includes many of the deep red states that supported Mr. Trump before. The Trump Administration has continued budget cuts to education and the elimination of at least 29 programs directly related to education. The cuts have included $8.5 Billion, which is a 12 percent decrease from a year ago. Also, the Trump Administration is planning to cut roughly $2.1 Billion from the Title II, Part A known as Instruction State Grants, which is a program that directly supports teacher salaries. That will likely affect nearly 35,000 teacher's salaries across the country. While this is happening, the Trump Administration is introducing private school vouchers into the federal budget, which would likely allow $5 Billion in federal tax credits. These measures seem to be designed to undercut public education. While this is going on, Mr. Trump is trying to channel $5 Billion to an obsolete and foolish boarder wall.

APOLLO:

Do you have any other concerns?

MISS RULER:

Yes, I do. In his inaugural address he said that our education system was flush with cash and that deprived students of knowledge. What a bazar statement. Like most of Mr. Trump's statements, it made no sense. Then he appointed Betsy DeVos, who has long been an adversary of public education, as the secretary of education. Even he calls her "Ditsy DeVos." Nevertheless, I thought that he deserved a chance. Was I ever wrong? There is no way I could support Mr. Trump for another term. After seeing him in action, I don't believe he is qualified to serve in any public office.

APOLLO:

So, it appears as though you would not support Mr. Trump going forward.

MISS RULER:

Never again for any office of any kind.

APOLLO:

How do you respond Mr. Trump?

TRUMP:

After all that I've done for the teachers and all that Ditsy DeVos has done for the teachers, I am surprised that any teacher would say such things. You said that Uncle Same picked these people. I'm sure that Sam has poisoned their minds. He's good at that. He's like fake news. He's never been elected to anything. What he says shouldn't count. He's just bad news. He should just go. Make him go. He's twisting these people against me.

APOLLO:

Thank you for your response Mr. Trump. Also, thank you, Miss Ruler. Now would the next person please step forward, state your name, and tell us who you are and why you are here.

At this point, Miss Ruler steps back a bit so that she is standing next to Mr. Big Jeans and is still seen in full light. Earnest Craft steps up to address Apollo.

EARNEST CRAFT:

For whatever reason, we union workers initially believed that Donald Trump was our friend. Were we ever wrong! He said that he would work hard for us and that he was going to help with wages. Every step of the way, Mr. Trump has done the opposite. At one point, he made it easier for Wall Street to undercut our 401(k)s. He has driven home the idea that the trade deficits were the fault of China and that we were losing jobs to China. Ironically, he and his family have many of their products made in China instead of the U.S. Here in the U.S. Mr. Trump has erased a rule that extended overtime pay to millions of workers. He and his administration have undermined safety rules at the workplace, including coal mines where he falsely stated that he would help. Additionally, he said that more miners would be back to work. That, too, proved to be false.

UNCLE SAM:

Has it been mostly a wage and safety issues with union members?

EARNEST CRAFT:

It's been far more. Mr. Trump has reversed a ban on toxic chemicals and that has a direct affect upon workers. He has changed the way work place injuries are reported. Workers compensation has been undermined. He has rolled back the regulations on payday loan sharks which has had a direct effect on workers. Employers are allowed to violate minimum wage and overtime rules. Child labor laws are being ignored and discrimination in the workplace has increased tenfold. He has done nothing to increase wages or sick leave or earned income tax credits. Plus, by his constantly trying to get rid of the Affordable Care Act, he is causing direct harm to the average worker. The frosting on the cake is the fact that Mr. Trump has done everything he can to destroy labor unions.

APOLLO:

Would you support Mr. Trump going forward? Vote for him?

EARNEST CRAFT:

No sir! I would never vote again for Mr. Trump. Never again.

APOLLO:

Do you have a response Mr. Trump? Here's your opportunity to clarify the record.

TRUMP:

This is starting look like another witch hunt. I've been the best President the workers have ever had. No one has done more for the workers than I have.

APOLLO:

Okay. If that is the case, would you care to elaborate?

TRUMP:

I don't have to everybody knows all the things I have done. I don't need to explain myself to anyone.

APOLLO:

If that is your defense, we'll leave it at that. Thank you, Mr. Trump and thank you, Mr. Craft. Who is next? May we have your name?

At this point, Earnest Craft steps back a bit so that he is standing next to Miss Ruler and is still seen in full light. Father Doubt steps up to address Apollo.

FATHER DOUBT:

Hello Sir. My name is Vasily Doubt. My ancestors were Ukrainian immigrants several generations ago. Partly because of that heritage and partly because of my chosen profession as a man of the cloth, I thought that Mr. Trump would be far different than he has been, especially in regard to religion and Ukraine. First of all, I was seriously mistaken by believing the relationship between the United States and Russia would improve. Naturally, I was concerned about relatives living in Ukraine. Instead of Mr. Trump strengthening our position with Russia, he has made a fool of us and has attempted to place the U.S. in a position of subjugation to Mr. Putin and Russia. That is all wrong. Because of my background and heritage, I believe the Russian people are a lot like us. However, the Russian leader Vladimir Putin is one evil and devious person. He can never be trusted. Mr. Putin is a real enemy of the Ukrainian people. Mr. Trump and his supporters have gone the wrong way. Instead of strengthening our position and standing against Putin and his minions, Mr. Trump has made us look weaker and stupid. The first sign should have been the rumors that were later confirmed that Putin's Russia was trying to help Trump get elected.

UNCLE SAM:

Wasn't there even a celebration of Trump's election on the floor of the Russian State Duma?

FATHER DOUBT:

Yes. It was the first sign that the rumors of Russian influence in our elections were true. I became so sick that I actually threw up. When I read the news that Mr. Trump and his administration tried to force Mr. Zelensky, the Prime Minister of Ukraine, to capitulate to a series of ridiculous demands in exchange for promised aid, I decided to come to this rally in order to ask a series of questions about the matter. I never got the chance and was shouted down when I tried to get some answers. That is counter to democracy. I'm convinced that Mr. Trump does not really believe in democracy. He wants to be a dictator, just like Putin.

UNCLE SAM:

So, is it a fair statement to say that because of the position that Mr. Trump has taken with Russia, you are concerned about him continuing as president?

FATHER DOUBT:

It's far more than that. For one thing, I didn't like the way I was treated when I stood up to ask my question. Mr. Trump berated me for being some sort of liberal plant. I seriously resent that. I would not allow myself to be a planted spokesperson for someone else or a cause. Certainly, not a liberal one. As a man of the cloth, I am quite conservative. I really resented being chastised in front of everyone and being labeled something I am not.

Additionally, there is a far more important reason. As a person of faith, I am very distrustful of a person, like Mr. Trump, who displays a total disregard for morality and the basic precepts of religious thinking. Mr. Trump has constantly berated people of faith. His attacking of immigrant communities of faith and people who are poor is totally unchristian-like. His attacks against people who are of different faith than his, whatever that might be, is getting very disturbing. When he used the National Prayer Breakfast to intentionally speak of a specific form of belief and purposely leave out other believers was evidence of his efforts to weaponize religion in a manner that brings forth the type of people who purposely target other religions and beliefs. Those actions are dividing this country and driving people against each other; all of which, is contrary to the Constitution of the United States, as well as, most religious principles. So, as a religious person, I can no longer support a president who purposely divides us as a nation. It is clear that he is using religion for all of the wrong reasons. I really resented him using the Bible as a prop in front of St John's. I am confident that I am on the side of the majority of citizens, the 60%, who say he is either "not at all" religious or "not too" religious. As I said, I resent anyone who uses religion as an excuse to get their way or to get votes. I can no longer support Mr. Trump and do not want him re-elected as President.

APOLLO:

Mr. Trump. Do you have anything to say in response to what Father Doubt has stated?

TRUMP:

Everything he said is a lie. In fact, I'm sure that I'm more religious than he is. Plus, he doesn't know the Russians like I do. They are good people and tell me what I want and need to know every time I ask them for help. Putin and Kisliak have warned me not to trust my own government. I certainly wouldn't trust some liberal priest. So there. This whole thing is worse than a witch hunt. You and Sam have set up a kangaroo court. You forget that I am President and I can do whatever I decide. So, what the priest says doesn't matter.

APOLLO:

Thank you, Mr. Trump and thank you Father Doubt. Now would the next person please step forward, state your name, and tell us who you are and why you are here.

Father Doubt steps back a bit so that he is standing next to Earnest Craft and is still seen in full light. Wilber Reeve steps up to address Apollo.

WILBER REEVE:

Pleased to meet you Mr. Apollo. I am Wilber Reeve. Let me start out by saying that I was one of the government employees who actually voted for Mr. Trump. Boy, have I had to eat crow. I have never seen the morale of government employees to be so low. It's not just Trump but his appointments that have been driving federal employees to the brink. The lengthy government shutdowns, especially with so many vacancies have seriously demoralized government workers. We blame Mr. Trump since it was he who could have and should have avoided the shutdown. Especially hard hit in terms of morale are the departments of Homeland Security, the Department of Agriculture, the Air Force, the Social Security Administration, the IRS, the Department of Education, the Justice Department, especially the FBI, and the State Department.

UNCLE SAM:

In addition to the low morale, isn't there a looming problem with the proposal by Mr. Trump to reduce the value of federal retirement benefits, which are expected to go down while the cost goes up?

WILBER REEVE:

Yes. Mr. Trump's latest budget would be more of the same in regard to his disregard for federal employees. In the past two budgets, Mr. Trump recommended pay freezes, although he ultimately agreed to nominal increases that didn't keep up with the cost of living. Plus, with the budget cuts to most agencies, the federal government will have difficulty functioning. He is also planning to use robotic calls instead of human beings; therefore, there will be additional cuts to the workforce.

UNCLE SAM:

As a result of what you have said, are you, as a government employee, comfortable with Mr. Trump?

WILBER REEVE:

Absolutely not. There are a few more items that I would like to mention. Under the Trump budget proposals, there will be fewer federal employees to help the public in various significant areas, including: the Environmental Protection Agency, when we are experiencing the worse exposure to our environment for decades, maybe forever; the Housing and Urban Development, when housing has become critical for the lack of adequate housing ownership and rentals; the Department of the Interior, as the Trump Administration tries to move public lands into the hands of the private sector; the Department of Transportation, when our highway and bridges are at critical stage; the Department of Labor, when we have the highest unemployment rate in many decades; the Center for Disease Control, while we are experiencing an awful pandemic, the COVID-19; and the Department of Education, while the United States keeps falling lower and lower in world education comparisons. Finally, from my perspective, it seems foolhardy for Mr. Trump to attempt to reopen the country and the federal government on a normal basis when his administration offers no guidance for how federal employees will be able to safely function in government workplaces during an epidemic. Why is he attempting to create a health problem for all of us? Why doesn't he work with health officials? Why doesn't he work with all of the governors? Not only will I not vote for Mr. Trump; but I will urge everyone I know to vote against him.

APOLLO:

Mr. Trump. How do you respond to what Mr. Reeve has said?

TRUMP:

I don't know this guy. I don't think I ever met him. He's got to be a plant of some kind. He's probably one of those disgruntled Democrats that just lives off the public funds. Pay him no heed. He ought to be thrown out. Just throw him out! That's it.

APOLLO:

If that's all you have to say Mr. Trump, we'll move on. Thank you, Mr. Reeve. I appreciate your comments. Perhaps we should now hear from the next person in line. You sir, will you tell us your name and provide your impressions of the rally and Mr. Trump.

Wilber Reeve steps back a bit so that he is standing next to Father Doubt and is still seen in full light. Four Seasons steps up to address Apollo.

FOUR SEASONS:

I am James Thorpe and I am a Tribal Leader of a Native American tribe. My tribal name is Four Seasons. I am a true Native American and have been politically active most of my life. In fact, believe it or not, I have been a registered Republican like many members of my tribe. Historically, and since the "Trail of Tears," imposed by President Andrew Jackson, a high percentage of Native Americans have historically been Republicans. Accordingly, we had high expectations for the Trump Administration when they came into office. Needless-to-say, I am both disappointed and disillusioned with President Donald Trump. Let me mention my reasons. My first disappointment came when I thought that the Trump Administration was going to protect Native American lands, which are only about 2 percent of the U.S. Mr. Trump and his administration have been trying to take away 56 million of tribal acres because of what are believed to be about one-fifth of the nation's oil and gas reserves. I view any efforts to take away this land for drilling and exploration purposes to be a violation of tribal self-determination and culture. It is a further effort by Mr. Trump and his administration to undermine Native Americans and to place our lands into the hands of the wealthy oil barons, who want to privatize our holdings.

UNCLE SAM:

Do you believe this effort by Mr. Trump serves to defeat the laws that keep Native American lands off the private real estate market?

CHIEF FOUR SEASONS:

Yes, I do. Apparently, the estimated $1.5 Trillion value of our reserves is too much for the Trump Administration and its money grubbing people to pass up. Unfortunately, Mr. Trump is also supporting the completion of an oil pipeline through a North Dakota Indian reservation. Mr. Trump has lied to us. I'm sure that other minorities feel the same way. Now, I have no idea why a member of a minority group would ever support Mr. Trump.

APOLLO:

Mr. Trump. Did you hear what this tribal leader has said? How do you respond?

TRUMP:

Far too much land has been wrongfully set aside for tribal use without consideration given the natural resources. The country needs these natural resources that are a benefit for everyone. The Indian tribes need to think about that instead of themselves.

APOLLO:

If that's your response, I can understand the disappointment and concerns expressed by Four Seasons. So, with this reason, I suspect that your people no longer support Mr. Trump.

CHIEF FOUR SEASONS:

Wait! There's more. Mr. Trump has also moved to restrict how the tribes in the United States can reclaim homelands via land trusts. His administration took the Mashpee Wampanoag land in Massachusetts out of trust; he tweeted about this matter while calling Senator Warren "Pocahontas;" he approved of reducing the Bears Ear Monument by 85 percent in order to open that area in Utah for oil and gas bidding; he decreased the size of the Grand Staircase-Escalante National Monument for similar reasons. These are matters that are illegal and beyond Mr. Trump's authority; he is allowing pipelines across native land; Mr. Trump has been cutting federal programs like the Supplemental Nutrition Assistance program that directly affects Native American children and families; his voter suppression laws are affecting Native Americans; and he insults us to our face while Native Americans are supposedly being honored for WWII code takers in front of a picture of the master of the "Trail of Tears," disaster, Andrew Jackson. I, for one, will not abide with such deceit. I will never again vote for Mr. Trump. He's not a good Republican. That is all I have to say.

APOLLO:

Thank you, Four Seasons. Oh, and thank you Mr. Trump for letting us know just how you feel. Now would the next person please step forward, state your name, and tell us who you are and why you are here.

Four Seasons steps back a bit so that he is standing next to Wilber Reeve and is still seen in full light. The next person to step up to address Apollo is Professor Probe.

PROFESSOR PROBE:

Thank you, Apollo. I appreciate having the opportunity to speak. I want to thank Uncle Sam for making me one of the persons to come forward. Presently I teach physics at the university where I am a tenured professor. During my time as a science professor, I have worked with many administrations and, in that regard, I have helped many other professors and students write their applications for various grants. Because of that fact, I have become familiar with many aspects of science, as well as, my own field of physics. Although I have tried to remain apolitical during my time as a college professor, I decided to get involved in the political world when the Trump Administration decided to turn its back on climate change.

UNCLE SAM:

Why did you get involved politically?

PROFESSOR PROBE:

For Mr. Trump to call climate change a hoax is a major blow to the intelligence of anyone who has a brain. Climate change is very real. Yet, when Mr. Trump became the president, he proposed to eliminate almost all of the climate change programs and he took us out of the Paris Climate Agreement. That agreement, which was signed by nearly 200 countries was a proper an ambitious action program to fight climate change. It was seriously needed since mankind was accelerating the destruction of the ozone layer, destroying plant life at an unforeseen rate, and animal life with more species being lost every year. Before Mr. Trump became President, the United States was a world leader. Now we are not leaders. Because of Mr. Trump removing us from the Paris Agreement, we are not even followers. Fortunately, he may not have the last say if we can get a new president in place as soon as possible. The agreement has to be in force three years before any country can formally drop out and then there has to be a year before a country can actually leave. Therefore, a new administration could foreseeably undue the stupid move by Mr. Trump in regard to the Paris Agreement. There is hope, but he has to go. We need a new president.

APOLLO:

Mr. Trump. Please feel free to provide your response.

TRUMP:

Tell him to go hug a tree. There is no global warming. It's a hoax and I've said that many times.

APOLLO:

Thank you, Professor Probe and thank you Mr. Trump for the two diverse views. Professor, would you please step back in order to allow the next rally attendee to step forward. Please identify yourself.

Professor Probe steps back a bit so that he is standing next to Chief Four Seasons and is still seen in full light. The next person to step up to address Apollo is Special Agent Jane Bond.

AGENT JANE BOND:

My name is Jane Bond and I am a Special Agent for the Central Intelligence Agency where I have worked for 17 years. I have been assigned to various locations across the globe and I am currently assigned to Langley, McLean, Virginia. Although I did vote for Mr. Trump for President, there is no way that I would ever do that again. It was within weeks of his taking office that I started to regret my decision. He has been the worst possible person to serve as President, especially when it comes to intelligence. It's as if he has no concept of the term. Since Mr. Trump took office, he has done nothing constructive for the intelligence community. He has tried to intimidate all of the intelligence agencies with his reckless and foolish conduct and statements.

UNCLE SAM:

What about Mr. Trump's ties to Russia and Mr. Putin?

AGENT JANE BOND:

Although I know my opinion is just that of one person; however, initially I believed that he was a compromised cut out. In case you didn't know, a cut out is a mutually trusted intermediary that would facilitate information between agents. At least, that's what I thought he might be at first. Now, I know better. With his pro-Putin, pro-Russia, and anti-intelligence community actions I am now convinced that Mr. Trump is, as the Russians call him, a "useful idiot." I say this because I don't think he is smart enough to be a cut out or a foreign agent; plus, I don't think that the Russians would be dumb enough to trust him at all. I sure don't. The extraordinary efforts that Mr. Trump has engaged in order to cover up his dealings with Mr. Putin certainly creates the impression of his being an agent of some sort. The Russian term of "useful idiot" is most appropriate and it bears repeating. Here you have a head of state who is either that dumb or an outright spy of some sort. Clearly, he is not smart enough to be a spy; therefore, he must be considered "a useful idiot" for Mr. Putin.

APOLLO:

I can understand your reasoning. Personally, I am familiar with Greek history and realize that the art of spying requires a certain level of intelligence; perhaps that is why it is called intelligence gathering. Now, from what I have heard so far from Mr. Trump in my earlier discussion with him and from what I am now hearing from those of you gathered here, I would have to agree with you that Mr. Trump is not smart enough to understand the intelligence process. Consequently, and from what you have said, I suspect that you no longer support Mr. Trump.

AGENT JANE BOND:

You have that right. I could never support Mr. Trump again no matter what he said or did. He has attempted to politicize the intelligence metrics and has ignored solid and repeatedly proven facts. By doing this he has undermined the ability of the intelligence communities, the elected officials, and the public from making objective and sound decisions about the valuable information that has been established from a multitude of sources.

Our job in the intelligence community, as trained analysts, is to provide sound, objective, and real information that can be used to make the important decisions that leadership requires. Until Mr. Trump came along, every president has supported the intelligence community and has, at least been willing, to read, assess, and understand the intelligence briefings and reports that have taken dedicated lives and efforts to compile. He won't even look at the reports or attempt to understand them.

Additionally, he has no sense of geography, history, politics, or the interactions of the various provincial interest of the people on this planet. Instead, Mr. Trump chooses to politicize all matters that come across his desk and bases his irrational decisions on the supposed "gut" feeling that he has at a moment in time. Finally, let me say that both the actions and the inactions by Mr. Trump in regard to the intelligence community and the information provided to him that has been ignored or misconstrued because of his isolated mind-set will have long term ramifications for the United States going forward. He should resign immediately. If not, he needs to be either impeached again or voted out of office as soon as possible before he does more damage to the United States. Please bring back the Pillars of Truth.

APOLLO:

What about it Mr. Trump? Would you consider resigning?

TRUMP:

Never in a million years. Why, I'm popular enough to be President for life. It would be the best thing for the entire world. Just think of it. Putin is going to be President of Russia for life and Xi Jinping is President for life in China. It's best for everyone if I'm President of the United States for life.

APOLLO:

Really? In any event, thank you Mr. Trump for your response to Agent Jane Bond. Also, thank you for your comprehensive statement Agent Bond. Now, let's hear from the next attendee of the rally. Would you miss, please come forward, provide your name and tell us about your reaction to the rally and Mr. Trump.

Special Agent Jane Bond steps back a bit so that she is standing next to Professor Probe and is still seen in full light. A young African-American lady steps up to address Apollo.

APHRODITE GAIA:

Hello, Apollo. It is nice to meet you. My name is Aphrodite Gaia. I work in the hospitality industry and have done so for many years while I have also been finishing my college education in social studies. I have to admit that I have never been fond of Mr. Trump. I never voted for him, nor, would I. I came to the rally to ask some questions about the outrageous conduct that Mr. Trump and his Administration have displayed when it comes to civil rights. More particularly, I wanted to ask some questions about how Mr. Trump and his Administration could justify their misplaced "photo ops" in front of churches and in churches after his administration drove peaceful protesters away from meetings designed to present a redress of grievances. It was both wrong and a violation of the law for Mr. Trump and Bad Barr to order police and troops to drive peaceful people away with rubber bullets and tear gas when those people were engaged in proper protest about a murder by police officers. I wanted to ask a simple question about that incident. I was never permitted to ask my questions and got the impression that I was not welcome at this rally.

APOLLO:

Thank you, Aphrodite Gaia. First of all, thank you for your courage in coming forward to a Trump rally and being prepared to ask a timely question of Mr. Trump. Permit me to also observe the outstanding nature of your name. As you know, Aphrodite is the Greek Goddess of love and beauty. Your family name also has great significance in Greek Mythology for Gaia was one of the original Greek Gods and the mother of all of life. You seem to be so appropriately named. I feel a natural bond with you. But, please continue telling us why you could not support Mr. Trump.

APHRODITE GAIA:

In regard to Mr. Trump and as far as civil rights are concerned, the list is endless and it continually cuts across ethic, religious, and financial standing. Just to highlight some of Mr. Trump's positions, permit me to mention a few: in 2017 he tried a Muslim ban, a consumer protection undermining, tried to eliminate deportation priorities, rescinded Title IX guidelines, ended a ban on private prisons, tried repeatedly to repeal the Affordable Care Act, tried to repeal the Fair Pay and Safe Workplace legislation, proposed tax reform for the wealthy, issued a hard line on deporting Central American children while separating them from their families; in 2018 he unlawfully required Medicaid recipients to be forced into labor. He rescinded payday lending rules, he implemented a race and ethnicity questions on census forms, he tried to roll back a rule that protects tip earners tip retention, he gutted the anti-lending discrimination laws, he delayed the implementation of enforcement of the act that protects individuals with disabilities, he issued orders to ban transgender people from serving in the military, he has issued a "zero tolerance" policy toward immigrants that separated children from their families, he instituted the longest government shut down in U.S. history; in 2019 he stopped cooperating with the U.N. regarding human rights violations in the United States, he proposed more money for the absurd boarder wall, he repeatedly undercut the role of independent regulators, he tried to deny health care to millions who are in marginalized communities, he stonewalled on the release of critical documents, he ordered the rounding up of migrant families, he moved to end asylum protection, he tried to cut over 3 million people from the nutrition program known as SNAP, he tried to deny visas to legal immigrants unable to prove they have health coverage; and in 2020 he undercut fair housing requirements for minorities and women, he tried to divert $7.2 billion of the military's budget for the crazy boarder wall idea, he tried to prohibit pregnant women from entering the United States, he tried to get states to cap Medicaid spending. I'm sorry to seem to ramble but I am only mentioning some of the many problems that Mr. Trump has created. If only I had been permitted to speak at the rally, I would have been able to mention some of these terrible transgressions by Mr. Trump.

APOLLO:

What is your response to Ms. Gaia, Mr. Trump?

TRUMP:

She obviously hates me. It's too bad that she doesn't realize that I have done more for minorities than any President in the history of the country. She's just like all of the rest of the dissidents that you and Sam have brought forward. It's obvious that you are trying to turn the people from the rally against me.

APOLLO:

Ms. Gaia, have I turned you against Mr. Trump?

APHRODITE GAIA:

No. He's done that to himself. Every day Mr. Trumps does more harm to the country and turns more of us against him. I will definitely do my best to campaign against him. I will now step back. Thank you for allowing me to speak.

At this point, Aphrodite Gaia steps back a bit so that she is standing next to Agent Jane Bond and is still seen in full light. A State Department official then steps up to address Apollo.

APOLLO:

You sir? I believe you are the final person waiting to speak. I'm listening.

SPECIAL ENVOY S.H. CONSULAR:

My name is S.H. Consular and I have been a career diplomat for the United States for nearly thirty years. During that time, I have served both Republican and Democratic administrations. About a year ago and for the first time in my long career I realized that the entire diplomatic corps of the United States was being undermined and disregarded by the person who should have had the closest ties to us, our own president. For the first time in nearly thirty years and probably the history of the U.S. diplomatic corps was there a total upheaval and a serious concern that the United

States was losing its respect world-wide. Out of the blue and after I had given a speech to a couple of universities of one of our closest allies, I was fired. There was no basis or reason given for the termination.

UNCLE SAM:

How about the budget cuts and the attacks on career diplomats?

SPECIAL ENVOY S.H. CONSULAR:

Right! There were the budget cuts, the hiring freezes, and the overwhelming personal attacks upon career diplomats by Mr. Trump has eviscerated the entire diplomatic corps and compromises the national security. To make matters worse, Mr. Trump has appointed incompetent and ignorant individuals to fill certain diplomatic positions. In some cases, he has appointed individuals like himself, who have no understanding or knowledge of history, world politics, geography, or leadership.

The entire State Department has become a total disaster since Donald Trump has become President. His appointment of political contributors and political hacks has undermined the Department of State beyond recognition. It is even worse for previously confirmed ambassadors who have returned from abroad due to the fact that if they don't find or receive another posting, they're required to retire. All of that talent and experience is being tossed so that Mr. Trump can continue to undermine and dismantle an entire Department of State that has taken decades to refine and establish. Initially, and after Trump started his reckless process of disrupting the State Department, there was a bit of a trickle of top talent departing; then it became a flood of career diplomats who have left thereby leaving the Department with novice replacements and a total lack of knowledge of what the State Department took generations to develop.

APOLLO:

I can appreciate your concern. With my knowledge of Greek history of ancient diplomacy, I understand you concern. Now, from what I have heard so far from Mr. Trump in my earlier discussion with him and from what I am now hearing from those of you gathered here, I suspect that you no longer support Mr. Trump.

SPECIAL ENVOY S.H. CONSULAR:

Good grief, no! Under Donald Trump the United States Diplomatic Corps has become known as the biggest international joke that ever existed. In virtually every foreign capital and country Mr. Trump is regarded as an inept clown. That's a double whammy if ever there was one. Although the foreign leaders and their countries have nearly universal distain for Mr. Trump, neither the country leaders nor their citizens are brave enough to express their true feelings for fear that Trump will cut off relations or aid or communications all together. Mr. Trump has made the United States the laughing stock of the world; and the very sad thing about it is that he is far too stupid to realize it. The best thing that could happen is for Mr. Trump to be soundly defeated. In my opinion, he has demonstrated that he is not competent to serve in any political office that requires the public trust. I came to this rally to see if there were any hope in salvaging his presidency and I can assure you that there is not.

APOLLO:

Mr. Trump. Are you listening? Do you have a response to what Mr. Consular has said?

TRUMP:

It's obvious that he doesn't understand diplomacy. That was the problem with the State Department before I became President. The whole diplomatic corps was a bunch of fools. All the countries of the world were taking advantage of the United States until I came along. I alone am fixing the world's problems. Someone had to do it and it's a good thing I became President. We're not being kicked around under my leadership. He's just a fool. Get him out of here. In fact, get them all out of here. Just like you, they're a bunch of fools.

APOLLO:

Thank you, Mr. Trump for your opinions, and thank you Mr. Counselor for your comprehensive analysis. Now, if you will please step back with the rest of the rally attendees, I will now speak with Mr. Trump and his remaining entourage.

As instructed, S. H. Consular steps back in line with the rest of the attendees.

APOLLO:

I want to thank each of you attendees for taking the time to provide your true feelings and why you will no longer support Mr. Trump. I am pleased that you complied with my requirement that you tell the truth. It appears that your opinions are right in line with my expectations; for you see, if it can be shown that there is a loud voice of the electorate and a mandate for the return of the Pillars of Truth, they will be permitted back into the United States. As you can see, I have already brought them back from Hell with the expectation that there will be a mandate for the removal of Mr. Trump from the office of President. I am satisfied that there is an overwhelming voice of the public against Mr. Trump and a mandate against his presidency. Now, and as far as I know, I have always been considered a fair-minded god; therefore, I will permit Donald Trump and his associates to speak in their defense.

Apollo raises his hand in the air, swirls it around a few times and motions to the Trump group to the right of the stage.

APOLLO:

You, Mr. Trump, and your associates may now add what you may please to your defense. As you have heard, when even the people in attendance at your rally must tell the truth, there seems as though there is a mandate against you. None of them will support you going forward and none of them will vote for you. What do you have to say about that?

TRUMP:

I'm not going to put up with this nonsense. I'm the President. I can do whatever I want. I want you, Uncle Sam, the Pillars of Truth, and that little guy in the drab outfit to leave now. This is the White House and I am the President who is in control. Don't try that trick to silence me again. Now, get out!

Trump and his associates start to move toward Apollo and the others, whereupon Apollo starts to laugh and again waives his hand in the air. When he stops Trump and his associates are locked dead in their tracks. They cannot move. Apollo smiles and speaks.

APOLLO:

From here on and until I decide otherwise, you, Mr. Trump, and each member of your entourage will be stuck in your present positions. You will be permitted to address me and answer my questions; however, you will be frozen in place for the duration of our discussions since I will not tolerate your walking around behind any of the individuals who attended the rally or anyone else, including me. Should you, or members of your entourage attempt to speak while anyone else is speaking you will be silenced again.

TRUMP:

What if I don't agree to this? I am the President of the United States.

APOLLO:

You have no choice. If you want to be heard, you will comply with my rules. By the way, I don't care if you are President of the United States. Presidents come and go by we gods are here forever. Now, do you have any questions or comments?

BAD BARR:

Let me handle this Mr. President. As the Attorney General, I will have you, Mr. Apollo, and everyone up here investigated. I will bring charges against all of you. I will see that each of you are indicted and prosecuted to the limit. In fact, with me as Attorney General, it will be beyond the limit. I've done it before, and I'll do it again.

APOLLO:

Really? What will you use for Justice since Lady Justice is a part of the Pillars of Truth and she is with me and will only be fully reinstated under my terms and conditions, which will be a mandate for the removal of Mr. Trump and his entire Administration, including you?

BAD BARR:

I don't care about Justice. The way I will handle this will be my way, and I will convene a Grand Jury. I will tell the Grand Jury to indict all of you at the same time.

APOLLO:

I'm afraid not. You will not be able to find me or the Pillars of Justice or Dearth during your final days in office. If you try to indict Uncle Sam, the entire country will know that you have finally gone stark raving mad. No one in their right might would even try to indict Uncle Sam. What will happen is that your term in office will end at the same time as that of Mr. Trump. Therefore, it will be after you are all removed when Justice and the Pillars of Truth will return under the mandate that I mentioned. You will appear to be even more of a fool than you are already.

BAD BARR:

I'll find a way to get you along with the Pillars of Justice and Dearth, too.

APOLLO:

No. Here is what will really happen. After the mandate by those individuals here on stage along with the rest of the public, you will initially fade away with a totally tarnished reputation. But you will meet up with Dearth again. You will meet Dearth when it is your time to make visit to see Hades. Dearth will escort you there. It will then be up to Hades as to what your fate will be. Dearth will return since it is not possible for even Hades to keep Dearth, the lack of substance, in the Underworld.

BAD BARR:

I'm through talking to you Apollo. I have nothing to say to you.

At this point, Bad Barr abruptly turns back to the right of the stage in a huff. Fruity Rudy then steps forward to confront Apollo.

FRUITY RUDY:

You can't talk to the Attorney General that way. It's not permitted. He's the top law enforcement officer of the land. He has the authority to enforce the law.

APOLLO:

I just did talk to him as I did. You know, there is nothing that you or anyone else can do about it. As far as his authority is concerned, he has no real authority without the Pillars of Truth. As I mentioned the Pillars of Truth will be back where they belong once the mandate that I am planning throws Mr. Trump and people like you and Bad Barr out of office.

FRUITY RUDY:

I don't care about the Pillars of Truth. They mean nothing to me.

APOLLO:

I know that. The Pillars of Truth mean nothing to you. They probably never did. Your behavior, especially in regard to the Ukrainian matter proves that.

FRUITY RUDY:

I am above the law, nine-eleven. I can do what I want, nine-eleven. I am known as the mayor, nine-eleven. I am a special envoy, nine-eleven. I am beyond your rules, nine-eleven. I don't need to worry about substance, nine-eleven.

APOLLO:

As usual, you make no sense. You are right about one thing though. You don't worry about substance and that is quite apparent. Therefore, you will be a perfect fit for Dearth when it is time for him to escort you to see Hades in the Underworld. I think that it is time for you to step back and contemplate, if possible, what you might tell Hades when you see him.

At this point, Fruity Rudy steps back to the right of the stage with the rest of the Trump entourage. Moscow Mitch then steps forward to confront Apollo.

MOSCOW MITCH:

Apollo, you may think that you are so smart; and I'm sure that you think that you can have your way with a couple of people who are appointed to positions. However, I'm an elected official. The people put me into office; therefore, I have special standing. I have significant power the others don't have. I control the legislation of the entire country because of my position in the U. S. Senate. If there is legislation I don't like, I kill it. If riders for a Bill come up that I don't like, I kill them too. If appointments come up that don't suit me, I kill them. If the House sends over legislation that doesn't benefit the rich or a private interest group, I kill that too. I have the power to kill and that is almost like the power of a god. In fact, I call myself the "Grim Reaper."

APOLLO:

If you think for a minute that the power to kill something is power like a god, you are more than sadly mistaken. The power of a god reaches far beyond the distasteful act of killing. You have such a distorted view that your unfortunate efforts have aided in the re-moval of the Pillars of Truth from the American public. It is that devious and malignant view of power that will surely grant you an audience with my uncle, Hades. It is my guess that he might even have a special place for you in the Underworld. In fact, as I recall, you consider yourself to be "The Grim Reaper" and have said so on many occasions. I'm certain that statement alone will amuse Hades. He is probably rubbing his hands together at this moment for the arrival of your presence. I'm motivated to put in a word for you with him. I won't be telling you what kind of word; but you can guess.

MOSCOW MITCH:

It is my expectation that he will like me because of what I have done, especially all of the pain and damage that I have caused to so many others. It is my guess that he will like me.

APOLLO:

I can assure you that you have guessed wrong. But I can tell you that you will be received with an eagerness by Hades that he has probably not had for quite some time. Keep in mind that Hades does enjoy his work. He also enjoys an amusing challenge. That is exactly what I believe he will find in you. I'm certain that he will be overjoyed when Dearth brings you to the Underworld. Please expect that Hades will have a special place for you. It is apparent that you have nothing to offer. You may step back until your time comes for Dearth to escort you directly to see Hades.

Moscow Mitch reluctantly steps back to the right of the stage with the rest of the Trump entourage. The cunning and arrogant FOX then steps forward to confront Apollo.

THE FOX:

Apollo, you might well have your way with the others; however, I am immune to you. I don't have to answer to you or anyone else for you see I don't have a soul. Therefore, I never worry about Heaven or Hell. When you are soulless like me, one never needs to concern themselves with the matter of ramifications one way or the other. I print and say what I like whenever I like it. I don't care two hoots about the Pillars of Truth. Truth means nothing to me. It never has. I'm in the business to influence people with propaganda and to make money, lots of money. I worship money and I like to tell people what to think in the process. The people hear my messages while I amuse myself when I see how stupid people can be when they literally accept at face value the total bullshit, I throw out there. I'm calling the shots. I have proven time after time that people will believe what they are told, especially if they are told the same unsupported swill that I present over and over. I am beyond your reach and beyond the reach of your stupid uncle Hades. Consequently, there is nothing you can do to intimidate me or to concern me at all.

APOLLO:

Oh, my goodness. What a clever and cunning creature. Have I met my match? Must I surrender? Whatever will I do? Listen you crazed entity. You are nothing more than a figment of the imagination of the devious and, perhaps seemingly soulless human beings that created you. What you have recklessly forgotten is that those individuals who created you and who may believe themselves to be soulless, are really not. I have them in my grasp and, more importantly, Hades will have them in his grasp. It is quite a grasp and the individuals who created you have no appreciation for what is coming their way. Hades grasp is one that cannot be broken.

Be assured that Hades has a special place for those who create a devious enterprise like THE FOX. There will be and are serious consequences for the purposeful misleading of both the innocent and not-so-innocent readers, listeners, and viewers of THE FOX. Payment must be made and payment will be made especially for the transgressions of those who try to hide behind artificial creations like media outlets in their attempt to escape accountability. There will be a big price to pay. Perhaps the creators of THE FOX believed that they had created something similar to Dearth. That is not the case. It will be Dearth who will be sent at the proper moment in time to escort the creators of THE FOX to their proper place in the Underworld.

Please be advised that I personally know that Hades has a special place for people of such deceitful and cunning deception. We spoke privately before my return today to the White House. Be assured that a most serious and permanent price will be paid. It will give Hades great pleasure to see Dearth delivering all of those who have used or attempted to use such deception, especially when it involves so many other souls. So, you see FOX, justice will be rendered after all. Your creators and perpetrators will never escape the clutches of Hades. Now, it is your turn to step aside while I address Mr. Trump.

The stunned FOX steps back to the right of the stage with the rest of the Trump entourage. Donald Trump is then asked to then step forward to confront Apollo.

APOLLO:

Now it is time for the featured personality of the unfolding controversies and disruptions to come forward to explain himself. Although I am sure that Mr. Trump will have an endless number of excuses and a multitude of diversions to throw at us, I am particularly interested in getting the Pillars of Truth back. The only way I see this happening is for there to be a public outcry and a mandate for the removal of Mr. Trump from office either through another impeachment coupled with a conviction, or a resignation from office, or the imposition of the Twenty-Fifth Amendment, or a mandate at the time of election, which, for various reasons, I see as the only realistic option. As I have set forth the options, let me first ask Mr. Trump if there is any chance that he will consider resigning.

TRUMP:

There is no way that I would resign. I am the greatest president the United States has ever seen. There has never been another president as great as me. No other president even comes close. In fact, we just had a rally here at the White House that was the first of its kind ever. Over 100% of the attendees are completely behind me.

APOLLO:

Hold on a second. Perhaps you are the greatest president in the history of the United States in the mind of a single individual. You. But that would be about it. Certainly, that is not a consensus. By the way, there have been many rallies at the White House. In the early days, there were not only rallies but inaugurations, as well. Thomas Jefferson's second inauguration was held at the White House. There were often open house events at the White House in the early days. At one-point Andrew Jackson had to leave for a hotel when about 20,000 citizens were celebrating at his inauguration on White House grounds. Even as late as the term of President Clinton there has been open house gatherings that many considered to be rallies. Finally, in regard to your reference to a mathematical percentage of people at your rally, the fact that you consider there to be a possibility to be an over one hundred percent factor explains quite a bit about your view of reality. In regard to the attendees of the rally to be over 100% behind you, did you just hear attendees tell us that they would never support you again for the office of President? Didn't you hear them say, they would never vote for you again.

TRUMP:

That's because you were twisting their words. They still love me. They know that I am a great president. That's why they are so loyal.

APOLLO:

It sounded like they each had a very good reason to no longer support you. In fact, I heard every one of them say that they would not support you. That sounded like a mandate against you. And, that is exactly what I expected. If there is a mandate against you, there is no way that you could be reelected. If you don't resign; or if you're are not removed under the Twenty Fifty Amendment; or if you are not convicted as a result of another impeachment effort, it sounds as though you will be defeated in the election by a mandate.

TRUMP:

You're wrong! I will win re-election and, even if I don't, I will not leave. If the election results don't give me the victory, it will be due to election fraud. I won't leave and there is no way for them to remove me.

APOLLO:

Does that mean that you will not follow the Constitution and the laws that require you to leave office if you are defeated at the election booth?

TRUMP:

As I said, there is no way I can lose. I am so popular. It's just like my television show. I am in control.

APOLLO:

What if there is a mandate? What if it is overwhelmingly clear that you have lost the election? What if you lose the popular vote by a significant margin and if you lose the Electoral College vote by an overwhelming margin. That would be considered a mandate.

TRUMP:

It would have to be a mandate that I could agree with; then I might consider going back into the lucrative businesses that I was in before becoming President.

APOLLO:

Well, and regardless of what you thought you heard from the people on stage who were at the rally, none of them said they would support you again. That seemed like a mandate.

TRUMP:

I'd have to hear it from more people. The people up here are the people who you influenced.

APOLLO:

Then let's do just that. Let's see what the people in the audience think.

At this point, Apollo turns to the audience to address them separately.

APOLLO:

Ladies and gentlemen of the audience, would you like to see the Pillars of Justice returned to the United States and released by Hades?

The audience overwhelmingly cheers in the affirmative.

APOLLO:

There you have it, Mr. Trump. The audience overwhelmingly wants the Pillars of Truth back. It sounds like a mandate to me. That is what I expected. Now, do you want me to ask the audience if they would like to see you removed from office? We can do a similar vote.

TRUMP:

Don't bother. It's obvious that you have rigged the audience just like the upcoming election will probably be rigged. I've had enough. You and everyone with you can go.

APOLLO:

Not yet. There is the matter of my Uncle Hades. I personally know that he expects you. He's even colored a replica of the White House in red for you.

TRUMP:

I don't intend to see your Uncle Hades. I have no desire to see him.

APOLLO:

I'm sure that is the case. However, because of all that you have done, especially to others throughout your life, Hades is expecting you. Please keep in mind that at some point, Dearth will come for you. When he does, you will be escorted directly to see Hades. He'll be expecting you. You may step back Mr. Trump and say nothing more or I will once again silence you. Now I will speak to Dearth. Dearth, at the appropriate time will you be prepared to escort Mr. Trump to see Hades?

DEARTH:

I will so long as I will be able to return. I have no desire to remain there.

APOLLO:

You have my assurances that you will not remain there. In my private discussions with Hades, while we were there, it was determined that there would be no way that Dearth, the epitome of absence or lack of substance, could be held by Hades or anyone else. You, Dearth, will be free to leave once you have completed your tasks of delivering Bad Barr, Fruity Rudy, Moscow Mitch, the principals of the FOX, and Mr. Trump to Hades.

TRUMP:

You can't make me go. I don't want to see Hades. I have no desire to go. Besides, I don't believe in Heaven or Hell. If I don't believe, then there should be no way that I can be compelled to go.

APOLLO:

It doesn't matter if you don't believe. That is the problem with individuals who have no conscious. But may be too late to develop one. It is you who have made it possible for you to meet Hades and suffer the consequences of you own actions.

TRUMP:

Will you please go? I've had enough of you. I don't want to see you or any of the others who are with you.

APOLLO:

Not yet. I assure you that ultimately, I will go. However, I must be sure that the mandate we have set in motion takes place. Once I am satisfied that such a mandate for your removal from office is in place, and that the Pillars of Truth will be back in their proper place as a part of the United States of America, I will go. To be sure, I must have the word of the audience that they will do their best to assure that a mandate for the defeat of Donald Trump at the next election takes place. Ladies and Gentlemen, will each of you do your very best to be sure that Donald Trump never again serves public office, including President of the United Srtates?

This is the time for the audience to give a resounding cheer of YES. Then the curtain closes on the presentation.

ABOUT THE AUTHOR

Richard A. Pundt is an attorney whose diverse career has included roles as a former special agent with the FBI, prosecuting attorney, special prosecutor, corporate counsel, trial attorney, and CEO of a tech company. He is the author of two legal books and a novel. Richard resides in Cedar Rapids, Iowa.